SAINT
Life from the kiss of death

SCOTT NIEMIC

COPYRIGHT 2018

Smashwords edition

"This is far enough, lads.

Kill the engine, and haul this soon-to-be-dead man out of my van.

And remind him to mind his manners, "a cheery voice said from the front seat.

Saint Sinner did his best to get his bearings. His head was woozy, like the day after a long night of drinking. In fact, it wasn't the drinking that caused his blackout. It was presumably what somebody had slipped into his drink that was the problem. Whatever it was, it hit him hard and took him down like a tranquilizer dart takes down a rhino.

His memory was foggy at best.

His recollection of the prior night was fragmented, bits and pieces coming together to form a distorted image. Something about a white van, but what about it?

He thought there was something odd about the white van. Something about it was off and seemed out of place. The more he thought about it, the more things began to fall in place. It still felt as if he was viewing the events of the previous night through a thick haze. He vaguely remembered seeing two strange men near the white van, painting a neighbor's fence. There was something about those two guys, too.

He didn't know what, but for some reason they were just as out of place as the van was.

What was it though? He just couldn't seem to put his finger on it, so he'd ignored the nagging feeling he had in his gut that told him something wasn't right.

After all, what was so strange about a couple butt-ugly guys working, painting his neighbor's... Just then he remembered what it was that struck him as odd about those two "painters."

Thinking back, as best he could granted the grogginess, aside from the fact that these guys didn't much look the part of your typical, everyday painters, he remembered seeing drops of paint all over the sidewalk. No professional painting company would be careless enough, sloppy enough to make a mess of the public sidewalk. With times being as tough as they've been, and the economy being shit, that would be reason enough for businesses to be on point. There was simply no room for carelessness.

That, right there, was a red flag. Ordinarily, he would have picked up on something like that. But, after the last few exhausting days of navigating back streets, exploring shady places, meeting unsavory people, and fulfilling his contractual obligations by eliminating predetermined targets, he was spent.

He was taxed, both physically and mentally, so much that his guard slipped, and he headed to a bar for a much deserved drink, despite the fact that he had quit drinking. Twice. In the past month. Never mind that, though, it was his birthday.

Friday the thirteenth.

Forty years had passed since his teen-aged mother had given him up to the Commonwealth of Massachusetts.

In his line of work, to live past thirty would be a blessing. The situation seemed to call for a celebration, so why not one for the road? This one, last time, for real. No bullshit. That's what he told himself, right before he headed over and walked into the Erie Pub, one of Boston's oldest Irish taverns.

That night the bartender had sent him a free drink, which he accepted. It was totally out of character for him to do so, but it was his birthday, and somebody did pay for the round. That was mistake number two. About three shots of Jamison later, he paid his tab at the bar before he left.

He hiked over to the intersection of Ashmont and Adams, to a mini-mart liquor store that was owned by a Greek family. The deli in back of the mini-mart was one of Dorchester's best-kept secrets. The drinking had made him hungry, so he ordered a steak bomb sub and an ice tea Snapple to go. Mistake number three. He never ate out. Being out in public was asking for trouble, an unnecessary risk, for somebody in his line of work. But, it was his birthday, right?

It wasn't like he had spent the entire night at the Glass Slipper, watching the girls up on the stage shaking their "money makers" or anything. Although, that didn't exactly sound like a terrible time, either. Maybe for his birthday next year.

He began to devour his sub. He took a swig of his Snapple and looked at the back of the cap so he could read the Snapple fact.

In the back of his mind he thought about where he might choose to live next, after this place. Just then, his legs began to feel weak, shaky. The Snapple fact may as well have been written in Chinese at this point, because there was no way in hell he could read what it said with his vision as blurry as it had become.

Everything faded to black around him. He felt like he was falling. Falling... That was the last thing he could remember. In retrospect, he had broken the golden rule: never expose yourself for too long but, he was a hard worker, and some jobs took more time than others to complete.

Regardless of however long it would take, he would never leave a job unfinished. Growing up, hard work, downing pints of Guinness, and taking pride in one's work was instilled into the young Shamus McGregor. He was proud of where he came from and never hesitated to lend a helping hand when needed. He was your typical, good-hearted Irish boy from the Boston area.

Snapple... it had to have been the Snapple.

Or maybe that steak bomb?

No, it was definitely the God-damned Snapple. As he sat, replaying the night's events, scene by scene, it suddenly struck him. Most, if not all, products come with a tamper-evident seal on them to let the consumer know whether the product has been opened or not.

For the life of him, he couldn't recall hearing the signature popping sound when he opened that damn Snapple. He remembered noticing at the time, but he shrugged it off and drank the refreshing beverage anyway. That had to be it. This was the kind of thing that led to him giving up drinking in the first place. Nothing stronger than lemonade, he had vowed. Yet, here he was again in the same predicament.

Getting sloppy and missing important details.

He had decided that when knocking off accountants, bodyguards, and under-bosses, he really couldn't afford to be sloppy anymore. It turns out, when you start taking people like that, people who belong to world-wide, notorious crime syndicates out, it doesn't take very long for the bigger fish, the guys at the top of the hierarchy, to take notice.

People like that don't appreciate it when their people start dying. In fact, people like that tend to get pissed off when things like that start happening. As a result, people like that tend to do crazy things in order to get their people to stop being killed off. Things like offering a ten million dollar reward, payable to anyone, for whoever is able to put a stop to the problem. In this case, Saint Sinner happened to be the problem. Whose problem, you ask?

Remember the cheery-voiced, older gentleman, with the Irish accent, who was seated in the front of the van? Bingo. He had personally offered the ten million dollar contract. Saint Sinner was sure of it.

So, it all came down to this... Killer's killing killers. Who was right, who was wrong? Good, bad? Which side was righteous, which was hell-bent?

That is the million dollar question.

The way Saint Sinner looked at it, there were two kinds of people in the world: Bad and Evil. Shoplifters, drug users/dealers, and the white-collar criminals, the fraudsters and immoral accountants who supplemented their bank accounts with illegally-acquired funds and those who fudged numbers and added a few extra zeroes to the end of their bank account totals: bad people, but not evil.

Ex-military snipers, recruited secretly and sworn to secrecy, hired for "shadow ops" and taking out targets around the world in the name of counter-terrorism and preventative maintenance. In other words, murder-for-hire. Hired by the alleged "good guys," though. Again, bad, not evil, right? Bad guys hired to do good, or good guys who are justified in being bad?

Hard to tell. Evil people, on the other hand, didn't care about the money, or whether what they did was for a good reason or not. It had nothing to do with the difference between right and wrong for them. Saint Sinner viewed evil as a sickness that people either had, or didn't have.

Saint Sinner was a bad guy, who made a living killing evil men. Evil men who harbored dark secrets. Some of the things these guys had done would put your modern-day horror movie to shame in comparison. We're talking about some real pieces of work here. These guys were comparable to Silence of the Lambs, as far as gruesomeness, but they lacked the same element of intelligence and psychological aptitude that kept people interested.

Basically these guys were known to torture their victims in cruel and unusual ways. Some of them at their very own twisted torture chambers located in the dungeon like basements of the private estates. Evil men, the heads of their corrupt empires whose goals are all the same: unlimited wealth and global domination. Evil men, not like Saint Sinner.

Not like most people.

Evil men.

Not only were these guys the cream of the crop but they also managed to make their way onto America's shit-list. It's no secret things need to be taken care of sometimes, and when that time comes, who do you call?

Someone like Saint Sinner, that's who. He is one of the best in the field, and he comes highly recommended.

His specialty is taking out politically sensitive targets who are connected to terrorists or terrorism, in one way or another. This is exactly why he currently found himself coming-to, bound in the back of the white van that belonged to those bullshit-painters that had struck him as being out of place in the first place, the night before. The voice in his head was loud, and it sounded like a disappointed parent when it said, "See what happens when we drink?"

They probably had been conducting surveillance and had an eye on him, since his Gulfstream touched down at Logan Airport. They were probably the type that had in-depth files on their targets.

Files that included everything you could think of, including your server's account of what you had ordered for dinner at the restaurant you went out to eat at the night before. Everything. These guys had most likely been watching, been waiting, and been planning exactly how they were going to intercept Saint Sinner for a while now. Probably even before he had left for L.A., a month prior, to handle the last contract he had accepted.

A kiddie-porn distributor. This guy was also linked to laundering money in Southeast Asia with representatives from notorious crime syndicates. Mr. Sotto was his name, and he was the recipient of one well-placed, high-velocity fifty-caliber round that was delivered, first-class, right to his dome.

After receiving the package, there wasn't much left of the guy from the chin up. It'll be a closed casket funeral for Mr. Sotto. That was just one evil man scratched off the never-ending list of shit-bags that needed to be dealt with.

There are so many that need to be handled, that when choosing a contract, you had to be selective and very particular. You want to choose a target that matters. Every hit needs to count. A good target is somebody that when taken out, will make waves in the water.

Someone that plays a key part in the grand scheme of things. Somebody, when removed, who will cause a void in the system. Someone the big guy at the top of the pyramid is going to hear about and be furious about losing. But, never mind all that. The point is, these guys were professionals. Once the drugs kicked in, it was a wrap. Down for the count and into the van.

There was only one man in the Western Hemisphere that wanted him bad enough and had the resources to accomplish a feat such as this. Surveillance. The hired goons, posing as painters. Simply being able to know the target well enough to successfully spike a beverage with drugs, with the fore-knowledge allowing for the right beverage to be chosen, and on top of that, having the target consume that very same, drugged beverage. All-in-all, it was rather impressive to think about. It was a perfectly executed plan. Had they wanted him dead on the spot, they very well could have killed him. The fact that he was still alive meant only one thing. They must have plans for Saint Sinner, something special in mind pertaining to how he's to be disposed of. But, for now, he was alive, and as far as he was concerned, that was a mistake on their part. Being blindfolded, gagged, and bound, there wasn't much he could do, but he was able to think about what he might do, if given the opportunity, so that's what he did.

Suddenly, the van skid to a halt.

He could hear dirt and small pebbles being kicked up and hitting the undercarriage of the van, as it came to a stop. Somebody killed the engine. Heart pounding, Saint Sinner was in survival mode. The years of rigorous training had instilled in him a sense of clarity, nerves of steel.

He took a deep breath and cleared his head as best he could. "Pull yourself together, this is it. No second chances here. Nobody is going to save you, but yourself," he thought. Just then, he heard a loud creaking sound as the doors in the rear of the van were opened behind him. Immediately, hellish-heat filled the air around him, hot and dry. Using the limited clues he had available, he desperately tried to determine where he might be. He definitely wasn't in Boston anymore, the heat and dusty, dry air told him that much. He had to be somewhere in the South. Or, maybe in the West. Thinking like that only led him to more questions, though.

How long was he out for?

One day?

Two?

A week?

Before he was able to come to a conclusion, the smell of cigarette smoke filled the air and distracted him from his train of thought. What seemed like a second later, he was being dragged from the back of the van by what appeared to be, two men with the combined strength of a bull and an iron grip.

Out of the van by what appeared to be, two men with the combined strength of a bull and an iron grip. Out of the van and on his own two feet, he heard someone say, "Vino?" and another man reply, "Yeah, boss?" the elderly man with the Irish accent was apparently the boss, and this Vino guy an underling. No doubt, he was one of the two guys who dragged Saint Sinner from the van.

"Please remove the blindfold and take the gag out of our friend's mouth. We're not uncivilized, now, are we lad?" the boss said. "No sir, not at all, boss," Vino said, his voice scratchy, grating. "But Vino, do be sure our friend here, understands just how important good manners are to me. Vasquez will assist you. Make sure things are made clear, and I mean crystal." Vino and Vasquez both replied, "Sure thing, boss" and "Yes, sir."

Saint Sinner, still as blind as a bat due to the hood that had promptly been pulled over his head at some point during his abduction, was still fully capable of hearing what had been transpiring around him.

He had been listening to the conversation between his captors the entire time, hanging on every word as if his very life depended upon it. He knew the blow was coming, but from which direction and where it would land was still a mystery to him. He tensed his muscles in preparation, but wasn't expecting what felt like a knee to the stomach.

It was a hard hit, and it knocked the wind out of him. Saint Sinner doubled over in pain, gasping, trying to catch his breath. The two henchmen got him back on his feet, standing him up straight. For a second, he was brought back in time. Flashbacks from a previous job in Iraq of all places, flooded his memory.

He remembered himself using the same exact methods, the same tactics, using fear to motivate his targets to cooperate. Being temporarily blinded adds a whole new element of fear to the equation. Sometimes the uncertainty, not knowing, makes things worse. Far worse. Tactics like these, yield results.

Saint Sinner was pulled from his not-so-pleasant, trip down Memory Lane by the sound of Vino's scratchy voice, "Let that be a reminder to you. Mind your manners, tough guy. I don't think you'll forget, but just in case…"

To Saint Sinner's left, he could hear fast paced, shuffling footsteps approaching. The footsteps stopped a second later, right next to where he stood, and in the blink of an eye, pain blossomed in his lower back. It felt as though he had been kicked hard by somebody wearing some sort of pointed boots. Cowboy boots, perhaps. Down, like a sack of potatoes, he went. That had to have been a kidney shot. He'd most likely be pissing blood for a week, if he even lived that long.

He let out a muffled grunt as he hit the ground, but refused to give them the satisfaction of hearing him cry out. He would not scream, even if he could, or beg them for mercy. That wasn't his style. He was a tough son-of-a-bitch, who knew he could take pain just as easily as he could give it. He could hear one, if not both, of the cronies chuckling as they picked him up off the ground for the second time.

Saint Sinner didn't know exactly what these guys had in mind, or in store for him, but he had the sudden feeling that it was going to be a long night. He knew that if their plan was to simply kill him, then it wouldn't be so simple after all. He knew they'd most likely drag it out and take pleasure in making him suffer.

Saint Sinner knew one thing for certain, and two things for sure. They most certainly didn't bring him all the way out here for a picnic.

If, for some reason these clowns didn't finish the job, and left him alive, he would be back with a vengeance, and would make it a point to personally execute each and every one of them.

Slowly, very slowly.

And, if these guys were incompetent enough to allow him to somehow escape, again he would be back with a vengeance, and he would make it a point to execute each and every one of them, just as slowly. But, in his heart, he knew that these guys had no intention of letting him live. Had they simply wanted to send a message, they could have used the damn telephone...

In Saint Sinner's world, the transition from night to day was instant. Blinding darkness was replaced by blinding white light, as the hood that had been pulled over his head, for however long it had been there, was removed. The sun's light was so bright, it was staggering. His eyes began to water profusely as they struggled to adjust to the illuminated environment.

Bathed in the bright light, it took him a few agonizing moments to be able to finally see, but it didn't take him long at all to feel the barrel of the gun that had been pressed against his back, right between his shoulder blades. At about the same time, Vino said, "No funny stuff, tough guy, you understand me?"

Finally Saint Sinner was able to put a face to this "Vino" with the grating voice that he'd been listening to. The two men locked eyes for a moment, each man sizing the other up. It may have only been a quick meeting of the eyes, but in that moment Saint Sinner seemed to be peering into the very soul of Vino. The intensity of the stare, the now hatred that was passed from his eyes and into the very being of the other man, made Vino feel very uncomfortable. Inferior even. Vino blinked once, then twice, trying to get the attention off of himself. The moment had passed, it was over. Saint Sinner now saw what he was looking for: weakness.

Based on his recently garnered information, his mind began to race to formulate some sort of plan that would enable him to take advantage of Vino's lack of self-confidence and mental prowess and ultimately save his own life in the process. Although Vino did have the gun that was pressed tightly against his back, and he most certainly would be nervous and unstable enough to pull the trigger at the slightest of provocations, so that put Saint Sinner in a very precarious predicament. It was a fine line, and he would have to walk it very carefully, if he didn't want to end up with anymore holes in him than he already had. Which, of course, he didn't.

Vino flashed a crooked grin, full of yellow, half-rotten teeth, and he grabbed ahold of the corner of the duct tape that had been placed over Saint Sinner's mouth, to keep the gag in place. He began to slowly, ever so slowly, peel back the tape. It must have hurt, being removed so slowly like that, but then again, that was the point. Vino seemed to be getting impatient though, and ripped it the rest of the way off.

Naturally, some of the skin stuck to the duct tape, and when he yanked it hard, like he did, some of the skin came off with the tape. Saint Sinner winced as the tape came off. He spat the gag out immediately and licked his lips, where the tape had been. He tasted blood. The gag hit the ground with a soft thudding noise and kicked up a little dust as it landed. He shook his head and spit a few times, to get the taste of blood out of his mouth, before looking out towards the horizon.

Waves of heat rose from the sand that had been sitting, cooking, all day in the blazing sun, and distorted things far-off in the distance.

Things seemed to shimmer, and it almost looked as though there might be an oasis, a refreshing pool of water, among the dunes. Saint Sinner knew better than that, though, it was a mirage, and he knew it. As soon as his eyes had adjusted, and he was able to see, he could tell he was in the middle of a desert. Which desert, though, he had no idea.

Just then he tried to bring one of his hands up, to shield his eyes from the brilliance of the sun, and at the same time to give himself a better view of things around him, but he had forgotten that his hands were bound by heavy-duty, industrial zip-ties. Needless to say, his hands weren't going anywhere.

He had to find a way out of these restraints. If he couldn't do that, he wasn't getting anything else done, and that meant he was as good as dead.

He started to do what he was able to do.

It wasn't much, but it was better than nothing and better than simply waiting around to die.

He started looking around for landmarks he'd be able to remember, in the event he was able to escape. He took in his entire situation, using any and everything at his disposal to gain an upper-hand. After he did a quick, mental recon, and all things were considered, two words came to mind-All bad.

Based on what he saw when he looked around, the acrid, desolate landscape, he knew that he had been taken somewhere far away, to a desert, most likely somewhere in the Southwest United States or in Mexico. The first place that came to mind was the Chihuahua Desert.

One hundred fort thousand square miles of nothing but sand and the occasional cactus. A true desert wasteland that spanned from Arizona, all the way through to the end of Texas and into the heart of Mexico, the land of the lawless, where the men were quick to kill and the women were even more so.

Things started to make sense, all of a sudden. The Mexican badlands would be a perfect place to bring somebody like Saint Sinner, somebody who needed to be disposed of. No worries, when it came to disposing of the body. No worries about civilians accidentally coming across the remains, not out here. No worries about having to deal with the authorities. A perfect place, indeed.

Saint Sinner took note of the single-lane, horse-trail-looking road that trailed off into the distance. It had to have been made for horses, or for donkeys, because it most certainly wasn't wide enough for two vehicles to pass side-by-side. And, judging by the looks of the trail, it wasn't frequented by vehicles at all. This furthered his belief that he had been brought into Mexico.

The heat was scorching, it had to have been well over one-hundred degrees in the sun. The sweat beaded on his forehead and slowly dripped down his face and off his chin. He was half-surprised to find that his sweat didn't evaporate before hitting the ground. In sweltering heat like this, it felt as though it might.

Everything about the environment, where Sinner found himself currently, was harsh and unforgiving. It was fortunate, for him, that he had been through rigorous training that included climate-based survival.

He was relatively experienced, when it came to being exposed to extreme environments. Being left in the desert, to fend for himself, wouldn't kill him. But, being left in the desert, to fend for himself with a bullet in his back could definitely be a problem.

As if to emphasize the point, Vino pushed the barrel of his gun a little further into Saint Sinner's spine. The gesture brought him back to his predicament, out of his mind and into the present. Just then, another man stepped out from the far-side of the van. He had been there the entire time, waiting and listening.

The guy was a giant, he was massive. He had to have been pushing damn-near seven feet tall. He looked like he could have made the cut the N.B.A.

Not only was he tall, but he had a chiseled physique. His walnut-colored skin looked worn, or weathered, but it was stretched tight across his muscular bulk. He was toned, cut, even. This man was in excellent shape.

He wore a western-styled hat, the ones you'd see country singer's wearing in their music videos, on his head and a button down shirt, blue, with a plaid pattern. He had straight-legged jeans on, and a belt with an over-sized buckle. Sure-as-shit, on his feet were cowboy boots. Now Saint Sinner knew where that kick had come from, he had been wondering about that…

"Vasquez," he thought, narrowing his eyes at the man.

Vasquez had cold, hard eyes, and a mean stare. The eyes of a killer, seasoned in the field. Saint Sinner had seen countless others with the same look in their eyes. He had killed countless others with the same look in their eyes as well.

He wasn't afraid of Vasquez, but he was wary. Men like him are dangerous, and Saint Sinner knew better than to disregard, or worse underestimate, a man like Vasquez. Being overconfident, to the point of being borderline careless, has been the cause of death to many a good man. As far as Saint Sinner was concerned, you could never be too careful. He wasn't trying to be the next fatality due to lack of attention to detail.

Vasquez looked vaguely familiar to him, but he couldn't place where he might have seen him before. Surely, he would have been able to recognize someone of that stature, had he seen him before. At least, he thought he would have, anyway.

The process of scouring his memory, in order to discover where, or when, it might have been that he had seen Vasquez before, was interrupted when another, third man stepped into Saint Sinner's line of sight. He could hardly believe his eyes. At first glance, anybody would have seen the grandfatherly, older gentleman wearing a white baseball hat and expensive-looking track suit, and thought nothing of it. But, that was just a façade, and Saint Sinner knew it.

Standing before him was a criminal mastermind, a living legend. This man was somebody important. Important enough to have the attention of mafias and cartels, alike. The man led the largest, and most notorious, crime syndicates in the North American continent.

A ruthless killer that started at the bottom and clawed his way to the top, using dead bodies as stepping stones on the path to power. He was infamous, a king of the underworld. He was a very thorough man, and preferred to handle certain jobs himself. If he was here, it meant bad news. Saint Sinner knew who he was, not by name of course, nobody knew his name, but by looks. He had only seen pictures of the man before.

People referred to him simply as "The Boss," and his reputation preceded him, wherever he went.

For a moment, only the whistling of the wind could be heard, as the Boss stood, staring at Saint Sinner. The wind was refreshing while it lasted, but it was gone just as suddenly.as it appeared. Instantly, the oppressive heat washed back over the group of men like a wave, a wave of discomfort.

Movement, in the periphery of his vision, caught his attention. He looked, for a split second, without turning his head, and saw it was nothing more than a tumbleweed that had caught on the short breeze and came to a halt, along with the wind that had propelled it. Without saying a word, the Boss looked off in the direction of the setting sun.

There was angry sort-of beauty in the sunset as it fell from the sky and, in its failing light, painted the world myriad shades of reds and oranges. There was nothing quite like it, especially here, in the desert.

Saint Sinner's mind started to wander. He couldn't help himself from thinking strange thoughts. Thoughts of the ancient civilizations, the Aztecs, Incas, and Mayas. Thoughts of human sacrifice crossed his mind. He found himself as being the human sacrifice, his death meant to alleviate the anger of the divine being. He shook his head, clearing his thoughts. It must be dehydration finally kicking in. He was rather parched. Clearly, his mind wasn't as sharp as usual. Not good.

The Boss stood, one hand in his pocket, and the other holding what had to be the most exotic-looking Desert Eagle that Saint Sinner had ever seen. This gun was a work of art. Not only was it silver plated, but it had a gold inlay, as well.

The handle too, was funny. It was crafted from fine ivory, no doubt it was carved from a very expensive, most likely illegally-attained, elephant tusk that had been imported from somewhere in Africa for an obscene amount of money. That was definitely the man's style.

The gun and the outfit made a very odd combination. Saint Sinner could see how, based on how the guy looked, it would be very easy to underestimate him, and he was sure that people had made the mistake many times while he ascended to the top of the food chain. Here he was, seventy-two years old, living like he's still in his prime, enjoying life and having fun, but still as deadly an adversary as ever.

Just as Saint Sinner had been lost in thought a moment ago, The Boss seemed to be lost in thought now. He was scanning the horizon, a serene smile on his face.

It was as if he had been taken by the beauty of the scene. It looked like, if he could have taken a picture, or better yet painted one.

Saint Sinner didn't know which was more disturbing, the look of rapture on The Boss's face, or the gun pointed at his own.

Al "the Boss" McCracken, wasn't your run of the mill criminal. If you put together a visualization, a tree-chart, of the hierarchy of global organized crime, you'd find The Boss at the pinnacle.

He's known as an apex predator, top dog, and feared by any and everyone who knew who, or what, he was. Rightfully so, too. He commanded the top players in North America as well as Western Europe. Some of the most notorious, organized killers, cut-throats, and contract thugs the world had ever known, with an iron-fist, no less, but anybody who was stupid enough to laugh at the absurd irony of the situation was taken care of, already long dead.

The Boss hadn't simply been handed his position, either. According to the rather thick file Saint Sinner had on the patriarch, he had risen to power the old-fashioned way. Like many others, he started living the life during childhood.

At a young age, he had already made quite a name for himself, as he quickly climbed his way through the ranks of his neighborhood street gang, back in Dublin.

He started out small, with menial jobs like running numbers for local bookies and miscellaneous side jobs. Of all the work he had been assigned, collecting debts was his favorite. Not only did he enjoy collecting unpaid bills, but he excelled at it also.

Because of his utterly ruthless nature, it wasn't long before word of his savage exploits had traveled to the ears of the right people.

The people who mattered and looked for qualities like that in a man when considering hiring prospective associates into the certified ranks of the underworld crime families and syndicates.

His reputation preceded him. Once people caught wind of him being on the payroll of any particular loan shark, it wasn't long at all before debt that had been written off, long before, and those guys who had seemed to vanish without a trace, when it came time to pay their bills, started to appear, and settle their accounts, out of thin air, like magic.

That fact, alone, gained him notoriety in the streets. The Boss quickly proved himself to be stand-up and business savvy. Representatives from the leading Irish syndicate had been keeping an eye on the young man who showed them promise and potential. Just like that, it seemed, the doors opened to him, and he walked into the big leagues. The Boss didn't bother with trying to get comfortable. He had plans, big plans.

He wasted no time, when it came to executing his plan, along with anyone else who happened to be in his way. He started killing his way to the top, one adversary at a time. On top of being a stone-cold killer, he was an exceptionally cunning, and brilliant, young man.

He knew his competition and made it a point to quickly ally himself with their enemies. He was a master of manipulation, and it wasn't long before he had the major crime families pegged against one another, in all-out open war.

He had whispered into the ears of the family heads, sowing the seeds of deceit and watching them grow into paranoia, jealousy, and rage.

When one family would fall, due to internal strife, he would appear with his own crew, heavily armed, to "recruit" whoever was left to his cause. He would pick up the pieces, from the aftermath of collapse, and place them into his very own puzzle. He made examples of those who refused his offer. He did not ask twice, and your first answer is your only answer, so choose wisely.

Another thing that set The Boss from the others was his insistence on being present for, if not carrying out himself, the executions of the unfortunates who happened to incite his wrath. Oftentimes, he would choose to oversee the killing not only to ensure the job was handled in a professional manner, but also to make sure the way in which the condemned were disposed of met the gruesome standards of The Boss.

By the year 1979, The Boss controlled the most, if not all, the business in Ireland, Scotland, and Wales. His influence had expanded to reach the United Kingdom and spread throughout most of Europe.

He even had ties in Eastern Canada, he set up shop in Montreal's Old French Quarter, and from there, and he slithered south and worked his way to the West.

He had engineered a fail-proof system, or so it seemed, to encompass all the vices. Prostitution, narcotics, gambling, and loan-sharking, he had his fingers into it all, but there was a balance. Interspersed, throughout it all, was a plethora of legitimate businesses that were meticulously managed and accounted for.

Dirty money was easily laundered and the entire scheme was vastly more successful than The Boss had expected.

The amounts of cash generated and controlled, by all the avenues he had operating, was staggering. Everything he touched seemed to turn to gold; a modern day King Midas. He literally had the luck of the Irish.

By 1983, he had the entire East Coast of the United States on lock. Every major American based, biker gang peddled his wares, helping him expand his reach not only up and down the coast, but Westward too.

Within a relatively short period of time, his influence spanned from the Atlantic Ocean, all the way to the Pacific. He was a regular at the Virgin Islands, and he used them as his getaway, treated them as if the islands were his personal marinas. He demanded respect, and everybody he came in contact with fell in line. His style was old-school mob, all the way. He handed out favors like a bookie hands out tickets. Everyone, from CEO's of multimillion-dollar companies, to politicians, to law-enforcement officials, even to the higher-ups of the government were indebted to him.

The Boss had come from the rough-around-the-edges, twelve year old kid who ran with his Dublin street gang, to the head of his own global empire, responsible for important roles in the importing, exporting, and distribution of tens-of-thousands of tons of narcotics annually.

That, alone, crowned him king, and made him the greatest, non-Hispanic, drug lord in North America. Consequently, that put him in the crosshairs of every cartel from Mexico to Argentina.

Asian organizations, who had their own gambling dens, brothels, and drug trade, didn't think very highly of The Boss and his associates and waged war as they vied for global domination. But, the Asians and the Central American cartels weren't the only organizations who paid attention to what The Boss was doing.

The National Safety Administration and the Department of Defense set a record when posting the reward for the head of The Boss. Eight figures, thanks to the deep pockets of the United States government.

The reward was bigger than that offered for the capture of Osama Ben Laden and James "Whitey" Bulger, combined. The wanted The Boss badly, and they were willing to pay an ungodly amount to have him taken off the streets, one way or another.

Saint Sinner remembered the day his contact had slid the contract on The Boss across the table and, literally, onto his lap, at the café, like it was yesterday.

It was right after he had amassed his one-hundred-sixty-third professional kill, while on active duty and serving his fourth tour of duty in Fallujah, Iraq. He had been two-weeks into, and eight days away from completion of, his tour.

He had been posted on a rooftop, around the clock, peering through an eight-inch hole and keeping watch over the half-mile kill zone in the shit-hole currently known as Fallujah, when he had received the orders stating he was to be relieved of duty. He hadn't requested, expected, or wanted for that to happen. He had wanted to stay with his brother-in-arms until the end, either until he was killed in action, or until he was on his way home, after the successful completion of his campaign. But, there he sat, across from his contact. "What's this?" he had asked, looking down at his package. The man across from Saint Sinner, whose eyes and most of his face lay hidden behind his aviator glasses, simply replied, "A career change."

The only thing Saint Sinner knew about his contact was that he belonged to one of those "hush-hush" divisions of the N. S. A. The ones that were classified and didn't really exist, spoken about only in whispers and kept in the dark, hidden from most. This man kept tabs on killers, snipers in particular, like a scout for college sports follows players.

He had an offer for Saint Sinner that he really couldn't refuse, an invitation to serve his country doing what he loved; killing bad guys, so he accepted.

The man explained to him that The Boss was the ultimate target, and there was an entire army between him and The Boss. The only way he'd be able to get close enough to the man would be to follow his example and work his way from bottom to top, killing anybody who got in his way.

The contact had related this job to the situation with Pablo Escobar. "Just like that," he said, "take them all out until you have a clear shot. And, by the way, we pay five figures, or better, per job." The nameless, short man in the gray suit could have fit in anywhere. Saint Sinner had no doubt that he'd forget his face the moment he left. They'd end his military career with an honorable death. He was sure there'd be a twenty-one gun salute, at Arlington cemetery, his very own fake grave site and stone, backwards boots on the horse, and all that other fancy stuff you'd see at a military funeral service. But, he wasn't dead yet, and he was trying to keep it that way.

But, that was long ago, and this is now. And, oh how the tables have turned. Now, the hunter had become the hunted. Saint Sinner, angel of darkness, who killed evil men, off the record of course, for the United States National Agenda, was, for the first time, both captured-and-standing face-to-face with The Boss. Two alpha males.

Two apex killers. One bad, the other evil.

Opposite sides of the same coin, and the currency was death. Both men seemed to be sizing one another up, there was nothing sentimental about it, and neither of them appeared to be overly impressed with the other. Now that Saint Sinner really knew the gravity of the situation, and who exactly he was dealing with, he had a little bit of a better idea as to where he was currently located. It turns out his intuition was, yet again, on point. He was somewhere in the Chihuahua Desert. It was rumored, well, maybe it's not so much of a rumor as he thought, that The Boss used this place as his own, private graveyard. In fact, he wasn't the first to decide this particular desert was an ideal location to off bodies.

This spot had been shown to him by a close associate, which is exactly why he liked to use it, and that was as close to sentimental as The Boss would ever get. It was all in the file that the Department of Defense had slipped him, unofficially, historic figures like Al Capone, Billy the Kid, and the James Gang were all said to have been linked to burying people and treasure, too, in and around this very same area back in their day. Train robberies, hold-ups, and wild chases with the United States Calvary were local legends in these parts.

Desolate land, torturous conditions, and isolating from the public and the law, made this place a haven for bad guys who needed to lay-low for a while. Also, in the middle of sniper training, there was always the debate between his fellow peers. Some said that there were ritualistic sacrifices made in the caves of this area. Something about honoring the gods and goddesses, the gate-keepers, of the lay lines, nodes where lines of longitude and latitude are in the right spot, together and opened a door to a parallel universe. A string theory shortcut, or so they said. A pair of mini-black holes next to each other, except they were made from white matter, they said.

Tribesmen and shamans alike had worshipped the same gods, in the same caves, for some two thousand years, or more apart, was proof. Pagans, Native Americans, and even Viking gothics had been to the spot and left their marks. The latter lovingly leaving rough looking slash marks, some people call them runes, one of the first alphabets to have even been used.

Sniper school had been rigorous, ruthless, but it had taught him a lot. His instructor had told him that talking was a way to keep the mind balanced, when you begin to feel the effects of severe dehydration. Desert acclimation training and his anti-terrorism training programs, both, required the soon-to-be snipers to go without water, to experience the delusions and hallucinations that accompany dehydration, so that if they were ever put in a situation like that, they would be able to recognize the sensations and deal with the problem accordingly. Proper preparation prevents piss-poor performance.

They were encouraged to keep a steady flowing stream of discourse to keep their minds busy, distracted from their thirst. Saint Sinner wasn't too sure about how well it worked, but he learned more than he thought he'd ever need to know. Then again, that was twenty years ago. A long time to forget things, to grow soft. But, fortunately for Saint Sinner, he kept up with his conditioning training.

His body was strong, solid, and he was as fierce as he had been, twenty years back.

The Boss and his two goons positioned themselves, along with Saint Sinner, in a crude semblance of a horse shoe around the back of the white van, its rear doors opened. Saint Sinner was still bound at the wrists, unable to stop whatever was about to happen.

He thought about partially charging them with a football style rush, maybe catch them off guard with that, and maybe karate kick one and roundhouse another, but he quickly discard the idea. He knew that would lead to a wild-fire of bullets, he'd end up with a bullet in his foot, or ass, maybe even one in the dick, instead of a clean shot to the head. On second thought, the idea wasn't very appealing, a shot in the crotch?

No thanks.

"So this is how it ends, a round between the eyes and call it a day?" he wondered.

He hung back, waiting, watching for them to make a move, to play their hand. He didn't plan on laying down and dying without a fight, but he didn't want to act too soon and lose any advantage he might have had by being patient. Besides, they had to have something in mind. If they were just going to shoot him dead, they could've done it and planted his body in the Charles River. Something had to give.

Vino nodded, it was like he was trying to suppress a grin. What the fuck was so funny, though? He passed Saint Sinner's elbow to Vasquez, whose catcher's mitt-sized paw clamped onto his forearm, without a word. He seemed to be recalculating Saint Sinner's every breath, his eyes cold, and his face expressionless. He looked like an evil Clint Eastwood, walking and carrying a big stick. He clearly, was the muscle of the group and was fairly intelligent, definitely the one to keep an eye on at all times. Fortunately, the last of the after-effects of whatever drug they had slipped him, were fading away.

Saint Sinner was able to think clearly again, and that feeling of swimming through mud had all but vanished, it had been tapering off while clarity and focus had been restored. But, the boss was also aware of the current situation, he stared at Saint Sinner and said, "Vino, why don't you fetch the gift for our guest?"

Vino grinned ear-to-ear, just like a kid at Christmas, "Sure thing, Boss." He reached into the van and picked up a big box. He set it back down, opened it, and pulled out a second, smaller, box. He spun around, box in hand, and held it up for Saint Sinner's inspection. It looked like it was big enough to hold a basketball, or something around that size, and had no writing on it anywhere.

Saint Sinner began to wonder what might be in the box, but that was when he realized there was thick, red liquid that dripped from the bottom, along the seams. The box was dark, and it was soaked.

Now, everybody was smiling except for Saint Sinner, who already figured out what was in the box. It wasn't rocket science. Again, he eyed the dark, thick-looking liquid as it dripped fat droplets, like tears of a giant child that fell to the ground only to sizzle, and roll a short distance before stopping to collect in the quickly growing puddle below.

His first thought should've been "what's in the box?" but Saint Sinner was no stranger to death and gruesome endings, so immediately he asked himself, "Who – is in the box?"

The Boss was a Kevin Spacey fan, obviously. Saint Sinner had seen that movie with Morgan Freeman and Brad Pitt, the one where Kevin Spacey has a delivery service deliver a box, dripping with blood, to both of the detectives. Morgan Freeman knew what was in that box. The audience, working the movie knew what was in there. Saint Sinner knew, too, but...Fuck! Who did he love, that they had gotten to?

Al, The Boss, stepped around, his back toward the setting sun. His face was shadowed, black as night. His white tracksuit, shades, made him look like the world's most dangerous retiree.

Vino, the human ferret, wearing his black fedora inched to one side, placed the box at Saint Sinner's feet, and then stood by The Boss, clearly satisfied with himself. He was nodding, as if he was playing catch-up on an inside joke, looking at the box, then to Saint Sinner, at Vasquez, and back at the box again, and then to The Boss, over and over.

For a moment, nobody spoke. A moment of silence. The box had the floor at the moment, it seemed. "Well lad, aren't you dying to know what's in that box?" The Boss said, a broad smile forming across his face. Saint Sinner shook his head. No, he wasn't.

The Boss darted a glance at his lackeys and then back at Saint Sinner. For not saying anything, The Boss was clearly understood. Then The Boss spoke, "Maybe I'm Spacey, and you're Brad Pitt, now come and ask me what's in the box, lad, just one time for old Uncle Al, make an old-timer happy. Ask me what is in the box…?"

Saint Sinner frowned, clearly not amused, and said, "I'm not playing along." He thought to himself, "That's exactly what he wants me to do. I won't do it!" But his mind raced ahead of his thoughts, he had one question on his mind: the obvious…

"Who is in that box?"

No sooner had he thought that, and Vasquez decided to help him play along. Vasquez pistol whipped Saint Sinner in the back of his neck, that sweet spot where your spine meets the base of the skull. The blow sent a shock wave through his reflexes, dropping him to his knees. Face-to-face with the wet cornbread square that looked like it came from a bakery. Plain, gray, a new smell tickled his nose, just as Vino said, "When Boss says play along, and you play along!" He was practically leaning over Saint Sinner, now.

The Boss stepped a little bit closer, and in what could have passed as a fatherly tone of voice, he said, "Maybe it comforts you to know, that at this exact moment, six o'clock, on the button," he looked down at his simple, yet classy timepiece, then back, before continuing, "a man, by the name of Jeremiah Brandies, is recovering a box identical to this one, right down to the contents inside.

Saint Sinner was running out of patience, itching to get his hands around any one of their necks. "Patience," his inner guru advised, "just keep them talking while we find a way out of this. He got his feet under him, and he pushed himself up, to a standing position, his wrists still bound.

He said, "Why would I care about some asshole who opens a box with the severed head of his wife inside? And, in case you didn't now, I have no wife, no girl, and no family. So, whoever's head is in this box ate a bullet for nothing."

The Boss snapped, "Head?" A satisfied look found its way to his face, as both his henchmen laughed right along with him, like two puppets with pulled strings. Vasquez gave a silent head-nod, but behind those eyes, Saint Sinner saw murder.

"Okay, what the hell is going on here?" Saint Sinner thought, as he looked again, down at the mystery box, then over at The Boss, who happily began to explain.

"I'm no angel, but give me a little credit, as I'm not a monster either!" The Boss said.

Saint Sinner shook his head and thought to himself, "Yes, yes you are! That's exactly what you are!"

The Boss smiled big and said, "Seven, now there's a movie. Hollywood got it right. Good actors, good plot, great ending, and the climax? Fucking spectacular! Especially if you watch it all the way through, uninterrupted. Isn't that right Vino?"

Vino nodded vehemently, as he said, "Oh yeah, it's top shelf!"

The Boss clapped Vino on the back and smiled. Then he said, "You know why I love that movie, lad?

Saint Sinner's eyes almost bulged, when he realized that he might know whose head was in that box, "Oh shit!" he thought, the emerald eyed bartender from the Erie Pub! That has to be it! A wave of deep-seated regret washed over him. Melancholy, in such a way it made him think back and regret every word he had said, and every smile he had aimed in her direction.

They must have noticed the friendly banter between the two of them, and now this poor girl's body, and the head it was attached to, before he walked into her work, were separated.

Flirting with the wrong man...He was a selfish screw-up, everyone he met ended up dying? Either by his own hand, or from circumstances related to his association.

He lowered his head, berating himself. Vino crouched down and flipped the top of the box open, and said, "What the... Was he hallucinating?" It's the blood, he thought, it had some kind of a power. He took a deep breath and began to exhale as he looked down, into the box.

"Happy birthday, lad!" The Boss announced, clapping. Vino immediately followed suit, clapping and looking like some sort of a seal soldier in an aquatic army. Vasquez just stood back, watching the procession of events with his steely-eyed scrutiny that made him the scary creep he was.

Saint Sinner anticipated seeing the pair of lifeless green eyes staring back at him, the mouth frozen, and wide open, in a gaping display of horrified shock. The shock brought on by a power saw doing its job, and working it's very through your neck, severing the head from the body. He expected to look and see, the familiar face of the prettiest barkeep in all of Dorchester. He could already hear her voice inside his head, screaming at him thinks like, "This is all your fault! And "Thanks a lot, asshole!" and "How were your free drinks?"

"What the fuck?" Saint Sinner couldn't stop himself from saying, as he looked down, into the box, and saw a birthday cake. Possibly the world's ugliest birthday cake, at that. It was frosted red on red, and had red icing-letters, written in what appeared to have once been cursive writing. The scorching heat had melted the icing, so what the writing said was still a mystery to him.

The cake, as a whole, was beginning to look more like a soup than a cake. It was a mess. The only remaining letter was still legible, was big "H" and everything else was just a big mess.

The whole thing was a bloody-red mess, but it definitely was not a head in that box. He was relieved as much as he was confused. He couldn't help but wonder why he ended up getting a shiner like that, if no blood had been spilled? It made no sense to him.

The feeling he had had in the pit of his stomach led him to believe that surely someone had been hurt, badly. Anybody who has spilled blood before is familiar with that feeling in the air, around them. It was intoxicating. Heavy, and dangerous.

This was the worst birthday surprise he had ever received in his entire forty years alive, and he had had some pretty terrible ones, in the past. But, this "Seven" themed box, in the middle of the desert, topped them all.

Saint Sinner narrowed his eyes, as Vino began to laugh a rough, grating laugh. Vasquez went as far as to plaster a fake smile on his face, a smile that didn't touch his eyes.

He hated Vasquez, everything about him. Especially his arrogant, cocky, mannerisms. He thought "if this prick doesn't take me out while my hands are tied, I'm going to enjoy killing that one. " But, Saint Sinner was beginning to feel like Vasquez had something other than the mercy of a well-placed bullet, in store for him, something dark. There would be no such thing as a quick or painless death, if Vasquez had his way.

"What, lad, did you expect something different?" The Boss said, with a smile, "Did you think I was a heartless monster?" The Boss shifted his weight to his other leg, still smiling, he continued, "I bet you thought I'd gone and snatched up the pretty, little mouse, who served you your birthday drinks the other night, did you not?"

The Boss shook his head and said, "You know, O'Connor's daughter Emily?" Saint Sinner set his jaw and gritted his teeth, but didn't say a word. "Oh I did give it some thought, don't get me wrong, but then I realized it would be such a waste of such a valuable asset," The Boss said.

Saint Sinner arched an eyebrow at that, a look of interest and slight confusion plain on his face. The Boss seemed to get a rise out of the look on his face, nodding, he carried on, "She's a perfectly good wench, who I can count on to get this job done, and done right. For example, if I ever decided that I needed to have something slipped into a drink, or if I need anything at all, for that matter, she'll be there to cater to my every whimsical fancy.

Saint Sinner shook his head, clearly disappointed with what he was hearing. The Boss's smile grew a little wider at that, and he said, "I realize, lad, that you only care for yourself, and that you're a big, bad, tough-guy contract killer and all that other nonsensical garbage that you attribute to yourself, and because of that, it would be doubly wasteful for me to have taken her out.

Utterly disappointed, Saint Sinner started connecting the dots in his mind, "So it was the booze, after all, I knew it. But Emily, really? I still don't know if I believe it. But, I guess, that would make a lot more sense than the Snapple being tampered with, that would take an unrealistic stroke of luck to accomplish."

Also, the Greeks who owned that liquor store, weren't affiliated with The Boss. As far as Saint Sinner knew, they ran in separate crowds.

The odds of the two Greek brothers taking orders from an Irishman, or anyone for that matter, were slim to none. But, then again, you can never really be sure about something like that. Especially in the underworld.

"Just stay cool, "Saint Sinner told himself. "Vasquez is just looking for a reason, any reason, to shove that pointed boot of his up your ass, and on top of that, the sun's going down."

"You're already up shit creek, without a paddle, don't jump out of the boat and make it worse. Save yourself the trouble, and play along," Vino said, seemingly trying to sound like a concerned friend, more so than one of his captors.

"Spare me your bleeding heart routine," Saint Sinner said, looking The Boss in the eyes, "according to the New York Times, you're responsible for the bombing of a building in Costa Rica. All that, to simply eliminate a rival of yours who happens to smuggle cocaine.

One, who just so happened to be running the major smuggling routes, underground highways and tunnels, that run all the way through Central America and into the United States, right past the southern bordering states, where Trump is building his wall at the moment."

Right then, Vino interrupted Saint Sinner, "So what? What's your point?"

Saint Sinner looked from The Boss, over at Vino, and back again before adding, "Twenty-three innocent people, civilians, died in that apartment complex, that day. And, *somebody*" he made it a point to emphasize the word, while maintaining eye contact with The Boss, letting him know, for sure, that he knew exactly what went down, "had to have paid off the authorities, because when the official incident report was released, the bombing was referred to as an unfortunate explosion.

"Eleven of the twenty three people that died that day were children." A moment passed before anybody spoke. The Boss broke the silence, a dark grin, from ear to ear, sinister in every sense of the word, "I guess I made those cartel fellows think twice about messing with an old man, like myself, now didn't I?"

His tone was matter of fact, and his voice was low. This time, it was The Boss's eyes that were narrowed. "Violence, in their mother's neighborhood, is a message they understand. Respect, even. War, sometimes, equals peace lad, you know that. Who exactly, do you think you're fooling now, anyway" You, single handedly, have killed more people than the entire National Guard has in the past ten years. I'm talking about the whole branch of the service lad. So, spare – me - the – tears for the children act. Now how about a slice of cake, for the birthday boy?'

"My pleasure, Boss, one slice of cake, coming right up!" Vino replied, starting to cut the cake.

"Saint Sinner shook his head hard, and said, "No, thank you. You know what you can do with that cake, don't you?"

Vino stopped what he was about to do, looking from Saint Sinner, to The Boss, unsure whether to continue. "Do I have to spell it out for you?" Saint Sinner said, a hint of a smile forming.

The Boss frowned, and started to walk around the side of Saint Sinner, toward Vasquez, who was currently making sure Saint Sinner was under control, thanks to the gun that was wedged firmly between his shoulders.

The Boss then said, "You have a bad attitude, lad. Alas, yes, I know exactly what I can do with it. I can share it with your loved ones. Oh wait, you don't have any family. Your whore of a mother decided that she'd rather play with her Barbie dolls than with you. She dropped you off, like a bag of trash, didn't she? Which, in the end, is exactly where she ended up, herself, dead."

The two men locked eyes, both smiling. One's smile was genuine, the other was forced. Saint Sinner's blood began to boil. If he was the incredible hulk, he would have, just then, turned into the mean, green, fighting, machine and crushed the old man like the cockroach he truly was.

Saint Sinner couldn't think of anyone else he hated more than he hated the miserable prick standing in front of him, right then. It hurt to hear, because it was all true. Apparently, he wasn't the only one who did their homework. The Boss, like himself had a collection about people's lives, like kids collect baseball cards. But, it was true, Saint Sinner's mother was dead to him, just like that awful cake was.

The Boss, Vasquez, and Saint Sinner, all watched Vino, as he whistled while he picked up where he left off. He carved a crude looking piece from the cake, dropped it onto a disposable, plastic paint tray, and waved it in front of Saint Sinner's face. It was about an inch, or so, away from his mouth and nose, so close, he could smell the sugary-sweet frosting.

The up-close and personal presence of food reminded him of how hungry he was, but no matter how hungry he was, he was resolved to not eat that cake.

As usual, everybody, with the exclusion of Vasquez, had a shit-eating grin on their faces. Especially Vino, who began taunting Saint Sinner with that damned slice of cake. He waved it all around, making airplane sounds, and brought it right back to under his nose, meanwhile, saying things like, "open wide," and, "coming in for a landing." Saint Sinner was not amused, or impressed, by Vino's antics.

Saint Sinner spit at Vino, once he got close again, hitting him square in the face and dripping from his nose. The world froze. Vino was momentarily stunned, he just stood there, his mouth ajar, as if about to say something.

The Boss looked on, tilting his head, watching the saliva gather at the tip of Vino's nose, waiting for it to slide down, and fall to the ground. Just then Vino recovered from his momentary stupor, he whipped out his forty-five caliber, and shoved it in Saint Sinner's face.

"Motherfucker spit on me!" Vino yelled, "Cock sucking, two balled, bitch-ass, motherfucker!

Can I shoot this asshole Boss?

Let me shoot this son-of-a-whore!

Please?

In the most fatherly way he could have, like a scout master teaching a merit badge lesson to his group of boy scouts, The Boss said, "No son, we'd better not stoop to his level," he looked over at the seething Saint Sinner, and then at Vino.

They looked like two junkyard dogs, nose-to-nose, about to tear each other to shreds. "And to think he goes by 'Saint' Sinner. That wasn't very saintly, now was it lad?" The Boss said, "This man has a chip on his shoulder, and bad manner to boot! Obviously he didn't have a proper upbringing with loving parents to teach him wrong from right.

So, no Vino, this one only had a junkie, who turned tricks for old Rocky Sanders, a.k.a. 'the Sword-man' or 'Sandman.' I don't know how he got the first, but the second he earned, for having the perfect heroin he sold. That's what people would say, anyway. I wouldn't know, I never used drugs myself, and usually just off junkies, when I know I can get away with it. They're a waste of life, in the truest sense."

Vasquez nodded, seemingly in agreement with The Boss. "Nope, lads, this fella, here, wasn't worth mommy's time, so, I guess it's up to us to play 'daddy" for a while, and teach him that it's wrong to spit in the face of his host, especially when all they were doing, was trying to show him some god-damned hospitality.

Apparently, your own daddy didn't care enough to show you...oh, that's right! You don't even know who your father is! Because your mommy was a junkie-whore! I have a guess at who it might be, though." He stepped a little bit closer to Saint Sinner, "Old Sandman" was a big fella, much like yourself. I saw a photo of him once, wasn't easy to get, mind you, I had to pay off a retired homicide detective, call in a favor. You know, most of the people from our time are dead, dying, or going crazy. You and old 'Sandman' have the same eyes, lad," The Boss grinned. "So tell me, how does it feel to know that your daddy was whoring out your mommy, all full of dope?"

In the blink of an eye, Saint Sinner dove towards The Boss, head first, a guttural roar coming from somewhere deep inside of him, primal rage had taken control of him. But, his charge was cut short. Vasquez, who was standing right behind him, had been waiting for him to do something like that, and, unfortunately, he reacted immediately. Vasquez hammered Saint Sinner in the back of his head with the butt of his gun, taking him down to his knees. Saint Sinner, panting heavily, through gritted teeth, said, "I'm... going... to... kill... you!"

The Boss appeared to be amused by the futile attempt made on his life, and at the ah-so predictable choice of words that followed that failed attempt. He laughed, saying, "If you could have, you would have, lad. Come on, now, up you go. It'll be dark soon, and we have a hike to take." The Boss started to walk off, following a trail that led somewhere to the South.

Once The Boss had gone a little ways, Vino swiftly kicked Saint Sinner, who was still recovering from the near concussion he had gotten a moment prior, in the gut, "Whoops!" he said, smiling his stupid smile of his. Saint Sinner stumbled in the wrong direction, but not for long, before Vino grabbed his semi-free arm, pistol still jammed into his back. "Hold him a second, Vino said to Vasquez, I need to get that thing out of the van." He walked over the van, and he pulled out a large canvas hockey bag. Something inside the bag was making metallic clanging noises. "Shovels, probably," Saint Sinner thought. Vino carried the bag in both arms, but his feet were free to kick Saint Sinner with, and so he did, right in the lower-back. "March!" he ordered.

That kick was a wakeup call of sorts, and as he moved forward, he swore to himself that he would remember to think about it later, when he was somehow ending Vino's life. But, as for right now, he was still alive, so he reluctantly complied and kept it moving.

Four shadows marched, single file, down the sloping desert trail. They made their own way through many cacti, the ones that look as if they're being held up by robbers, you know, hands in the air, as the infamous Boss led them along, and almost cheerily he had a spring to his step.

Small, matchbox car-sized reptiles zigzagged from rock to rock, dashing underfoot, pausing briefly to roll an eye around before scurrying off, under the cover of shrubbery that had thorn-filled tangles.

The minutes felt like hours as they continued their journey. Progressively, the terrain changed. Small rocks turned into larger rocks, and those turning to boulders. The path itself became treacherous, stories that could easily sprain ankles were strewn about, and sand pits made for slow-going. The whole ordeal upset Vino, he continued to prod Saint Sinner with the barrel of his gun, and complain while he did it. "Move it, asshole!" Vino demanded, kicking Saint Sinner again. Saint Sinner smiled, on the inside, through the pain, because he knew that karma was a bitch, and that Vino definitely had it coming.

Vino seemed to be having a hard time keeping up with the brisk pace that The Boss had set, that was why he kept messing with Saint Sinner. It gave him a chance to catch his breath, and it made him think he was earning his way into The Boss's appreciation by roughing up the captive. "Slow down again, and I'll shoot you in the foot, I'll shoot your toe off, how's that sound?" He asked, huffing and puffing, "You want to lose a toe?"

Keep moving.

"Hey Vasquez," Vino said, "Why did you say we had to worry about this guy? He's not that tough, if you ask me." The Boss stopped for a second and looked like he was about to say something, but decided against it and kept going. Vasquez smirked at Vino, then glanced over at Saint Sinner, chewing the stub of his Camel cigarette.

The look on Vazquez's face told Saint Sinner everything he needed to know. He had just let him know that he knew Vino was the weak link in the chain. It also told Saint Sinner that it was almost that time. Time to say goodbye to this world, and everything in it.

The look on the face of Vasquez was somewhere between "you and me have some unfinished business to attend to" and "I've read your resume' of death, now let's see if you're the real deal." The Boss moved with a nimbleness that belied his age.

The Boss was in excellent physical condition, aside from his slight limp, you'd never believe the man was seventy-two years old.

Saint Sinner had picked up on the limp right away. He always paid attention to detail, but he doubted that either Vino or Vasquez even noticed that their boss favored his left leg. That just goes to show you the difference in the level of professionalism between Saint Sinner and your everyday goons.

The sun was hanging low in the western, afternoon sky. The brilliant reds and oranges, from before, gave way to shades of violet, across the darkening horizon. The desert sand sparkled in the last light of the day, bright colors being reflected here and there. It looked like it had rained diamonds, instead of water, down on the plain, and there they sat, just waiting to be plucked from the Earth by the greedy, grasping, fingers of man.

Saint Sinner took a deep breath, captivated by the beauty of it all, then let it go. He decided it was as good a time as ever to make peace with himself. "It's a good day to die," he thought. It all made sense to him now, why killers, in the past, would go out of their way to make sure the job was done or choose this place to make their last stand. It was so beautiful here. The sky was a canvas of color, and the desert was an ocean of brilliance that glittered under the first stars of the soon-to-be-night and the moon was already hanging low and rising.

Saint Sinner took a mental picture of the magnificent landscape before him, blinking in and out with each step.

It was something his mind has always done automatically, storing the photos for a dark time of need. The ways things were looking, such a time could be right around the corner.

"Almost there, lads," The Boss announced, like an evil tour guide. The boulders were clustered closer together, as they began to descend, down the canyon's gradually sloping wall. Larger, now that they were closer, they could see the openings in the face of the mountain. The entrances to caves, no doubt, varying in size. Some were only the span of a few feet, others were gargantuan.

These caves looked like they could've been dwellings from long, long, ago. From the Bronze Age, maybe. Ruins, waiting to be found and used once again. They seemed very similar to Colorado's Mesa Verde's Anastasi tribes, cave-dwelling people, who made homes out of the natural rock-face cliffs, carving out housing complexes that would protect them from predators and the elements, all in one. Anybody seeking shelter would have jumped at the chance to live in these caves.

The Boss called a stop to the march in front of one of the largest openings, it was easily thirty feet across, "this is it," he said. "Vasquez, keep an eye on our guest, while Vino fetches a spade from the bag." Vino looked confused, "A spade boss?" The Boss shook his head, disappointed, yet again, he said, "Vino, Vino, Vino...," he smiled.

"If your father hadn't shown me devotion and loyalty, like he did, back during prohibition, I would have had you put down a long time ago." Vino's eyes lowered to the ground, "I'm sorry, Boss."

The Boss said, "Yes, you are. However don't apologize, not for your own stupidity. Listen to me, you dim-witted fool, it's obvious that we can't have him dig his own grave with his bare hands.

The stone would be very difficult for him to get through with only his poor hands to do so, though I admit, it would be entertaining to see him try."

The Boss looked towards Saint Sinner for a moment, perhaps he was entertaining the idea, "Alas, we don't have time for all of that." He looked back at Vino, then to Vasquez, "But while we're here, boys, we're going to hook two fish at once. There's something I want to check out inside this cave. There's an old legend about some rubbish the History Channel was talking about, claiming ancient powers and the like. Just an outdated rumor, no doubt, but this is it. I'm not getting any younger. Even, I, know my time at the top of the cash pile, is limited. If the rumor proves true, I'll turn this place into my own, personal Disney Land. More importantly, though, it will put an end to my wondering about the whole situation."

Saint Sinner thought about the chink in Al's armor he had discovered: he was superstitious, then his eyes fell upon the cave's entrance. Vino said, "Well excuse me Boss. Wouldn't treasure hunters, like those old school pioneers, mountain men, or those gold-fevered miners have gotten ahold of any treasure lying around by now?" Nodding, The Boss replied, "Nobody's going to leave a big score sitting around for centuries, but this isn't any normal treasure. It's a doorway of some kind, a portal, they said, a gateway to another time and place.

Stonehenge, the Bermuda Triangle, the pyramids, the fountain of youth, that sort of treasure. A node. Their latitude and longitude holds astrological significance, according to those two atom smashing idiots at C.E.R.N. Lay Lines, this is a place like those. It's hidden inside somewhere. Unfortunately the men who stumbled upon that tip all had accidents with knives, while sleeping in their beds. Crazy coincidence, and messy.

Vasquez?'

"Yeah, boss?" Vazquez turned his attention from Saint Sinner to the Boss, awaiting further instruction.

"Be on point, it's about time we get started," the Boss said, looking at Vino, he added, "Vino, let's get started." Vino dropped the canvas bag, unzipped it, and from inside, he produced two shovels, a pickaxe, and several flashlights. Next, out came the Coleman Lanterns, and a bundle of rope. Once done unpacking, Vino pulled his forty-five from the holster on his hip and pointed its barrel back at Saint Sinner.

"Now lad," the Boss said, stepping in front of Saint Sinner, looking at him directly, "Let me make things crystal clear for you, before we begin our fun adventure. Vino?" Vino perked up.

"Yes, Boss?"

The Boss continued, "Didn't you always dream of becoming a surgeon, back when you were just a wee lad?"

Vino smiled at that, "You bet I did, Boss, I used to pretend I was a doctor all the time. It has been a very long time, though. I could definitely use some practice." He unsheathed his knife and made exaggerated zigzagging cuts through the air, all the while, a youthful gleam in his eyes.

The Boss nodded, looking back at Saint Sinner, he said, "Get my drift?" Saint Sinner nodded, then looked up at the sky one last time before they decided to drag him into the dark confines of the cave. He saw a red tailed hawk riding the currents in the air. It circled three times before it flew off the North.

That had to have been an omen if he ever did see one. He decided to continue biding what little time he had left, quietly. He figured if he remained quiet and withdrawn, they would believe him to be defeated, and resigned to his fate.

"Now," the Boss said, "do you want to work, or die?" as he smiled his signature white, toothy, smile. "Make no mistake though, either way you choose to go, you'll be dying, but one option will allow you to keep sucking air for little while longer."

It almost sounded like they were discussing a casual business agreement, and in a way they were. How did Saint Sinner want to spend his last moments on Earth? Digging his own grave out of the unyielding sandstone under his feet, or lying dead, his body cooling while the pit was dug out for him?

He was tempted to tell them all to fuck themselves, to let them slave in the heat to hide his mutilated corpse, but he knew that would only hasten the process of his demise. He could beat them, but to do so, he would have to remain cool, calm, and collected.

"What's it going to be lad? Daylight's a burning', the Boss said.

Saint Sinner knew that The Boss was a sadistic bastard at heart, and was the type of guy that read books on the Spanish Inquisition's torture methods, back in medieval times, just too simply broaden his wicked horizons. He needed more time. He needed to get free. That meant he needed to play ball. "I'll work, just make my ending a quick one, once the time comes, that's all I ask," Saint Sinner said. "I'm tired of this world, anyway.

The Boss squinted his eyes, staring at Saint Sinner, as he calculated a dozen different plans for what would come next. Saint Sinner had no doubt that The Boss knew of his extensive military training. He, no doubt, knew that Saint Sinner was almost as deadly unarmed as he was with a gun in hand. He – did - know, and The Boss would be watching him closely. Especially with this sudden change of attitude. Saint Sinner wouldn't be getting over on him again, The Boss thought, as he watched the bound man attempt to appear as though he had no will left to live. This man had become a serious fucking problem in the past few months. Thirty four of The Boss's underlings had met their end at the hands of Saint Sinner.

Men, who had made The Boss rich, running his rackets all across the globe. Finally, The Boss had found it impossible to carry on business as usual. He had to handle the problem, and here he was sitting in front of him, ready to die.

"That's a good, lad, "The Boss said, holding the gaze of Saint Sinner, his grin returning. "I knew you'd say that. But, know this, your little plan won't be working. You can buy yourself a little time, but you can't afford to buy back your life."

Both Vino and Vasquez stiffened at hearing The Boss's last remark, as if the thought had never crossed their minds. "It's okay though," The Boss continued, "by yourself the time. Lie to yourself, convince yourself that you're good enough to pull off a daring escape, one last time. Please, there's nothing I love more than watching the death of hope in a man's eyes when he finally realizes that the end has come. It's like a recreational drug to me, lad, it gets me high."

The Boss walked around, to the other side of Saint Sinner, "I know all about you, lad. Army ranger, and not just the point-and-shoot type, either. An intelligence officer, smart, and useful, enough to be recruited by the N. S. A., to run a division of the organization, once your contract was up. You turned it down though, didn't you? Wanted to continue doing what you really enjoy, killing. You certainly have a knack for it, and a style I can't help but admire. A real workaholic, but, unfortunately, you work for the wrong side.

That must be how you rationalize living the type of life, lad, by thinking you're working for the 'good guys.' Well, let me tell you, sonny, they're more corrupt than I ever was! The blood money they collect, from oil alone, makes my operation look like a lemonade stand.

You and I, we're not so different.

You're a killer for hire. For the past eighteen months, you've been taking out my upper-staff, hoping to get a shot at my handsome face. Ah, lad, you've been like a wolf in the hen house.

That last one you killed really got my attention," The Boss laughed, crazily would be an understatement, "sending a bullet through the only gap in a solid steel door?

Genius!

You planted that mother fucker right in Big Timba's brain. Somehow, you discovered his habit of verifying the faces of his visitors, himself, through the peep-hole. Even, I, overlooked that! Bravo!"

The Boos shook his head, "if the situation was different, "he looked almost regretful. "I'd pay you whatever you asked to have you work for me, but after all this ruckus, I could never let you get away with it.

Not to mention, I'd never be able to trust you. And, the hundred million dollars, on my head, is just too much of an incentive. Not that anyone is capable of pulling off such a feat. I've already made sure that anyone that could even come close to succeeding has been taken care of. Some people are too stupid, or too impulsive for their own good."

The Boss took a moment to read Saint Sinner's face. The lack of surprise, at the mention of the bounty, confirmed The Boss's suspicions. Only a few in the world, could offer such a high bounty. The list was incredibly short, the N. S. A., M16, or potentially some D. O. D., rehash cover, but it amounted to the same thing.

Far above, in the sky, another red tailed hawk called out. Saint Sinner looked up just in time to catch it circle around once and move on. A slight breeze could be felt, coming from the cave's entrance. That told Saint Sinner that there had to be another entrance to the cave in front of him, somewhere.

"Vino?" The Boss changed tact.

"Yes, Boss?" Vino replied, kicking at a lizard, but the little lizard was too fast for him.

"Cut the ties on our friend's wrists, and do be careful. Also, hand him a shovel," The Boss ordered.

Vino was face to face with Saint Sinner, but only for a moment, but it was long enough for him to whisper, "I'm going to use my scalpel, first, to operate on your eyes. That'll make things more interesting, huh? You'll never know what I'm going to operate next!"

Saint Sinner nodded slightly, and took a mental note to definitely kill Vino first, and to use his own knife to do it.

The ties were cut.

Saint Sinner rubbed his wrists, where the ties had been letting the blood flow back into his hands, as he watched the laser pointer circling on the zipper of his jeans. "Don't worry, I'm N. R. A. certified," Vasquez said, nonchalantly, as he set his sights on Saint Sinner's family jewels. "I'm great with moving targets, too, thanks to my dad. He taught me a coin trick when I was a kid.

He would flip a silver dollar up high, over his head, and with a .22 rifle, I was expected to hit the coin, dead-center. "In God We Trust" was supposed to take a perfect semi-circle around the entry hole. I practiced for years, from age seven to fourteen, before I hit my first bulls-eye. There's a certain knack to hitting a moving target, I'm sure you know that, though.

I saw all those marksmanship medals you had on your dress uniforms in your downstairs closet."

Saint Sinner maintained a flat affect, not letting Vasquez know that he was surprised to find out about the scumbag being inside his townhouse, poking through his wardrobe.

In his wardrobe hung seven custom-tailored Brooks Brother's suits, all ironed and organized by day of the week he would wear them. There was also his formal, green dress uniform, for parades that he hadn't worn since his last trip to the White House, to consult with a friend, who called in a favor, on a security matter. The same friend that lined him up with his last mission.

He filed that thought somewhere in the back of his mind, as he thought about that day after 9/11, when in-house killers were all suspect until they could figure out who the mastermind behind the attack, was. They pinned it on camel-riding, towel headed bad guys who shit in the desert and wipe with their bare hands. Ones who slept in caves and bounced around from village to village.

Foreign.

Different.

They were strangers in a strange land, invading holy lands like the Knights Templar, thousands of years ago. And, these sand dwelling tribesmen were still there, warriors in their own rite.

They were just scary enough to convince the American people that few Middle-Eastern rebels, now called terrorists, were responsible for the greatest attack on America since Pearl Harbor. It was the videos on the internet, of United States citizens being beheaded, that really sold it, though.

The general public fell for the story hook, line, and sinker. They ate it up, and worked themselves into a righteous fury, ushering in a new age of security, which gave the national agency carte blanch, and a never-ending budget to play with.

Overnight it seemed, the N. S. A., and the C. S. S., the Central Security Service, were abounding in wealth and opened doors.

The videos, promoting the "Death to America" theme, went viral, and stirred up every John and Jane in the United States. They took the attack personally, hatred welling up inside them, as they shouted dumbly at the aggressor, the target that had so conveniently been pointed out to them.

Meanwhile, the real evil geniuses behind 9/11 were just getting warmed up. That was exactly why he had set the trap. Saint Sinner highly doubted that The Boss had friends in his network, especially friends that deep in the mix, but, the M1-6 contact was close enough.

And, now, this cowboy with a death wish just received the distinguished honor of being made-man number two. Saint Sinner would be showing this man no mercy when the time came to delete him from the face of the earth, right after Vino was taken care of, of course. He might even use the same knife on both clowns.

"Here you go," Vino said, handing Saint Sinner the shovel, "where do you want the grave at, Boss?"

The Boss looked at Vino, rolled his eyes, and said, "Grave...," he chuckled, "don't be so dramatic. Right where he's standing is a mighty fine place, just as good as any other, I suppose. Vasquez, just keep that thing pointed right where it is," he gestured to the gun in Vasquez's hand, then nodded toward Saint Sinner, "and, if he so much as blinks in an aggressive manner, well, pretend you're duck hunting and he's the first mallard of the season."

The Boss grinned, and Vasquez nodded, "Yes, sir." Turning his attention back to Saint Sinner, The Boss continued, "Now, would be a good time to start digging, lad, if you stop, even for just one second, I'm going to start counting.

For each second of rest that I see you take, I'll be increasing my number by one. If, it so happens, I reach the number ten...Believe me, you'd rather not know that I will be granting Vino's wish, and allowing him to practice being the surgeon he always wanted to be."

The Boss winked at Vino, and Vino smiled a sinister smile and said, "You know, I could probably manage to string out your death for at least a day or two, maybe even three because you're a strong one.

A man can endure a lot more pain when he's a tough guy. The human body is far more resilient than most people believe, do you have any idea how long it'll take before your organs start to fail?" vino looked over at Saint Sinner, apparently waiting for an answer to the rhetorical question. After about thirty seconds, he continued, "Me neither. We'll know soon enough, though."

Saint Sinner said nothing. He just listened to all the nonsense, in one ear and out the other. He decided to get to work, stabbing at the hard, crusty-top of the desert floor. He swung the shovel around and discarded the heap of sand and rocks somewhere to the side. He was digging his own grave, and he knew it, but it had to be done.

In the meantime, in between time, he would be plotting and planning, scheming a way to turn the grave he was digging into his captor's grave, instead of his own.

The Boss's henchmen took up positions on either side of him as he slowly chipped away at the appointed task at hand. Their eyes were focused, and their trigger-fingers were ready. Ready to kill.

The Boss stepped closer to Vasquez, leaned in, and whispered something in his ear. Saint Sinner couldn't hear what was said, but The Boss looked appeased, and he started to whistle. It sounded like it might have been an Irish folk song, as he casually walked away, toward the cave's massive entrance.

The Boss set foot into the cave, his head looking left, right, and all around, trying to use the last of the failing sunlight to his benefit, trying to take in the scene around him.

The sand was still hot as hell from baking in the cruel sun all day long. The heat emanated from it, causing Saint Sinner to drip sweat profusely from the exertion of digging that damned hole nonstop. It dripped into his eyes, stinging, and into his mouth.

As time elapsed the strange sphere in the sky had finally found its resting place, below the horizon. Fortunately, for Saint Sinner, with the sun down, the temperature started to drop slightly. It wasn't much, but he was grateful for it. Stars began to twinkle and shine, in the twilight sky, and the nearly full moon was breathtaking. With the moon as big, and as bright as it was, it was still easy to see everything around him. It wasn't dark enough yet to warrant a flashlight.

The Boss had been gone for a short while now, and was presumably far enough out of earshot. Saint Sinner knew the time to act was upon him.

He needed to pick a fight with the two minions before he dug too deep and ended up stuck in the hole he was digging.

He needed to take their minds off of him long enough to make one good shot, one that counted. He would make sure it did, too. His life depended on it. In his mind, he was trying to determine which of the two were the weakest. At first, he had thought Vino, but now, he wasn't so sure. They both had their own strengths and weaknesses. Saint Sinner was running out of time and needed to make up his mind. Who was it going to be, Vino or Vasquez?

"Which of these two clowns would be easier for me to get worked up into a shit-fit" Saint Sinner thought, looking back, over his shoulders, as he shoveled his way closer and closer to his own demise.

He decided that there was really only one way to find out, "Vino...," he said, "don't let The Boss go too far all by himself. The legends are about evil spirits who inhabit these caves. They're true, by the way, and he's more than likely in danger right now. But then again, I'm sure a cultured man, like yourself, already knew all that.

Vino glanced toward the cave entrance The Boss had entered, a nervous look on his homely face. The Boss was clearly not in sight, he was somewhere in that cave, searching for God knows what.

Saint Sinner started counting, in his head, as soon as Vino turned to look for The Boss. Once Vino had brought his attention back to Saint Sinner, four seconds had elapsed in total. So, Saint Sinner figured that left a solid two-second, window for him to have done whatever he had wanted. He could do a lot with only two seconds. But, was he sure of himself, or simply overconfident? The Boss allowing him to be untied-and-giving him a shovel, which could easily be used as a weapon, increased his odds of survival by about eleven percent, or so, he figured. That, added to what he had already estimated his odds to eat, put him somewhere around the fourteen percent mark.

He'd have to move very fast.

"Hey Vasquez, what's a smart man like you, doing, pulling low henchmen duty for a senior citizen, like The Boss? He's looking to retire. There's no future with him," Saint Sinner said, watching him out of the corners of his eye, and waiting for some kind of reaction or response. But, Vasquez didn't take the bait. He didn't even blink. "Well that settles that,"

Saint Sinner thought, "Vino, it is."

He looked over at Vino, wiping the sweat from his brow, and said, "Vino, do you realize that Vasquez is going to have to kill you sooner or later, right? When The Boss retires, like he's already been talking about, you'll be done, too. Last time I checked, there was no retirement plan for low-level coffee fetcher, like you, once he sells the farm and moves into the bad-guy retirement home, of his choice.

Vasquez, here, will be his guy, and his first order will be to silence any weak links that could potentially connect him to his old criminal enterprises. Anyone who knows the intimate details, on any of the dirt, has to go. You know, things like where The Boss lives, stash houses, contact names, or really any information that could be sold and used against him if, let's say, somebody offered you a billion dollars to turn on your boss."

Vino just smiled at Saint Sinner, shaking his head. "Nice try, nobody would ever pay a billion bucks for The Boss. Not even for the president. Not for anyone!"

Saint Sinner scoffed, "Oh yeah? Then what do you think about the one hundred million dollar bounty that's currently being offered to anyone willing and able to put an eighty-six cent slug into the old man's skull? It's open to all takers, even you! All you'd need to do is dump a couple into him, and then head to the bank to cash the biggest fucking check you've ever seen."

Vino snapped, "Bullshit!"

Saint Sinner shook his head and continued, "That's enough for you and me to split evenly. Fifty million dollars each. We can split it. I'm a man of my word, Vino. I'll take you to get your money, myself.

Hell, the people I work for will pay you for offing the top target on their list. You'll see millions more in contracts, before the day is even over. You could work fulltime for them. Think about security! What I'm offering you Vino…Fifty million dollars in cold, hard, cash. All you have to do is shoot the Marlboro man, here, in the head. We'll go and get The Boss together!

That is, unless you want to keep being his bitch, and getting paid next to nothing, until he has you dig your own grave because you know too much for the old man to play shuffle board with a clear conscience.

You're just a worm to him. He's going to toss you out when he's done with you, Vino. I can tell. He won't do it personally, of course. He'll have Vasquez, here, cut your throat, or blast you in the back. Look at his face, Vino. It's all true! It's true, isn't it Vasquez?"

An uncomfortable silence filled the air, as Vino looked back and forth, between Saint Sinner and Vasquez. For a moment, the wind picked up, and with it, came a light dusting of sand that covered everything in their vicinity with a coat of light-colored, fine desert sand.

Vasquez kicked one of his boots against the other, in order to clear the sand that had amassed, meanwhile, staring through narrowed eyes at Saint Sinner.

Time was running out. The hole he was digging was already almost as deep as he was tall. Saint Sinner scooped another small pile of dirt and rocks into his shovel, making the pit deeper, still, he tossed it aside, and slyly said, "I give you another ninety days, tops, Vino. Once I'm dead, it's over for you.

You heard The Boss, he said it himself, and he knows his time at the top of the game is over. Guys like him are very thorough, believe me, Vino. I've been taking them out professionally for years now. Bad guys, like him, are all the same. They don't take chances. They kill people that know too much. Especially errand boys, like yourself, that don't bring in the big bucks for The Boss. You don't add zeros to his bank accounts, unless, of course you take into consideration the money you cost him, but those are zeroes in the wrong places.

Now, point that pistol at Vasquez, the-real-threat, and pull the trigger! I'm trying to save your life, man! Fifty million dollars, Vino! Kill him, Vino! Kill him, Vino!" Saint Sinner emptied another shovel-scoop, as he watched Vino process the information, he could almost literally see the wheels turning in Vino's head, fear and panic kicking in, confusion plain on his face.

Vasquez had had enough. "Shut the fuck up!" Vasquez spat.

That was the cue Saint Sinner was waiting for, "You see, Vino, he doesn't want you to know! Ask him! Look into his eyes, look at his face! Ask him if The Boss ever told him to be ready, whenever necessary, to snuff you out and throw your ass into an unmarked, shallow grave, probably somewhere right around here. Shit, this hole I'm digging could easily fit two bodies into it, now that I think about it. I have a gut feeling, Vino, and my gut never leads me astray."

Vasquez's blood began to boil, "I said, SHUT THE FUCK UP!" he yelled.

"Ask him Vino!"

"Just ask him!" Saint Sinner prodded.

Vasquez narrowed his eyes even more, set his jaw, his mouth was a thin line. He refocused his sights on Saint Sinner's crotch, trigger finger itching.

Vino's gun wavered, slowly sinking, lower and lower. He looked over at Vasquez, a strange combination of dismay and courage on his face, but most of all, he looked hurt.

Vino turned, fully facing Vasquez, now. He took a deep breath, to steady himself, before pointing his forty-five at Vasquez, all of a sudden sure of himself, "Is it true? I need to know, Vasquez, don't fuck with me!" Vino's voice was all accusation, "Huh! Did you and The Boss have a conversation about clipping me, once he retires? Is that what you two were doing down in Fort Lauderdale, is that why he bought the warehouse there? Huh? Answer me!"

Vasquez shook his head in a disgusted manner, "Why you dirty son-of-a-bitch!" He was glaring at Saint Sinner, if looks could kill, they would have.

"Answer me, god damn it, is it true?!" Vino shouted, his hands shaking.

"Yes, Vino, it's true! Look at him! It says it all over his face, he's about to kill the both of us! That was the plan, this whole time!

What do you think The Boss whispered in his ear before he strolled off, all of a sudden so happy he was whistling? He wasn't whistling so that I wouldn't hear what he said, he didn't want you to hear him dead men tell no tales, Vino! Now shoot his ass, before he shoots you!" Saint Sinner said, practically begging Vino to do something, pretending to sound as desperate as he could.

"NOOOO!" Vino screamed.

Vasquez had just enough time to readjust his gaze, from Saint Sinner to vino, before Vino started unloading his clip, into him, hitting him twice, out of the eight shots fired. Vasquez lay sprawled on the ground, as Vino continued to pull the trigger, a click, click, clicking, and sound coming from the spent clip.

Vino shook the gun, as if to hear if there were any more bullets rattling around inside the gun, before he lunged at the prone Vasquez, climbing on top of him and beating him to a bloody pulp, all the while, screaming things like, "that is what he whispered to you!" and "kill me?!" and "who's smarter now, asshole?"

Saint Sinner swiftly grabbed the spade, holding it with both hands, like a baseball bat, and swung it with every ounce of strength he could muster, at the back of Vino's neck, while he was till preoccupied with Vasquez's beating. The shovel connected with Vino's neck, squarely separating his head from his shoulders. The second swing hit, with a sickening thud, bone crunching and blood spraying.

Vino's lifeless body landed on Vasquez's cooling corpse. Saint Sinner rolled Vino over and relieved him of his knife, then he located Vasquez's revolver, moving as quickly as he could, just in case The Boss was on his way back. He was sure that The Boss had heard the shots.

Saint Sinner knelt down, partially hidden by the two bodies. He went to lick his lips and realized that his face, shirt, arms, hands, and everything was covered in Vino's blood.

Saint Sinner shook his head, thinking to himself, "I can't believe I just ingested some scumbag's blood... Almost immediately following that thought, he was overcome by a strange feeling that someone, or something, else was looking through his own eyes.

It felt like he was momentarily sharing his mind with another person. He tried to shake the feeling, but nothing seemed to work. He had more important things to deal with, currently, than a strange feeling, so he checked the revolver, to make sure it was fully loaded, and grabbed a flashlight from the canvas bag. Turning the flashlight on, to make sure it worked, he headed for the entrance to the cave. He was on a mission. He had a score to settle, he needed to finish this once and for all.

It was time to hunt down The Boss. The tables had turned, thanks to a trigger-happy, insecure bad guy, and, now, it was time to track down the top dog. This was it.

The moon was still high in the sky, and very bright, so Saint Sinner was able to use the moonlight to make his way up to, and into, the cave without needing to use his flashlight right away.

He didn't want The Boss to know exactly where he was by giving him a bright-ass light to use as a target. The Boss had to have heard those shots, right? He would know that something had gone awry. The sound from those shots would have traveled for miles, and in the confines of the cave, the noise would have been amplified.

"So much for an ambush," Saint Sinner thought.

He had six shots to tear the soul out of the old bastard who deserved a much slower and more painful death than a bullet could offer. Saint Sinner would use his own hands to do the deed, if he thought he could get away with it. But, he didn't. Better to just shoot the old fuck, and be done with it. "Now, to find that miserable old prick," Saint Sinner thought. He looked around, and back behind him, and noticed the white van. The van was behind him, so that had to mean The Boss was still somewhere deep inside the tunnel network of the cave.

There was a chance the old man had found the other entrance to the cave, but Saint Sinner doubted it. The Boss was just a seventy-two year old man, who was lost in the cave, unprepared. It wouldn't take Saint Sinner long to find him, or so he thought.

He zigzagged his way deeper into the cave, a short burst here and there, from one side to the other. He paused for a moment, hunched down in the dark, with his flashlight and gun at the ready. He took a few deep, slow breaths and continued on his way deeper into the cave. The cave appeared to be made from sandstone, the walls felt smooth and the roof of the cave looked smooth, too.

As he slowly made his way forward, he hoped that luck was with him, he did not want to trip and fall down a crevasse and end up breaking a bone. It was dark, really dark. He held his hand in front of his face, and couldn't see it at all. He had a sneaking suspicion that he'd end up walking into an ambush. He was thinking about how far he'd come, and how much it would suck to end up dying now.

Saint Sinner got to his hands and knees, to reduce the chance of being spotted if, for instance, the old man heard something and shine his light to investigate. His groping fingers felt along the floor. Smooth, just like the walls. It almost had a man-made feel to it. Saint Sinner's eyes were finally beginning to adjust to the dark. He was now able to make out vague shapes in the darkness around him.

He noticed the ramp-like floor of the cave descending down, down, into the darkness. He also took note of the general shape of the cavern he stood in. But, the one thing he was looking for, The Boss, was nowhere to be seen. He was definitely around, somewhere, though. Now, that, Saint Sinner knew for sure.

Now that his eyes had adjusted, he scanned his immediate area for some sort of a clue, and to where the old man could have gone. In doing so, he though he saw something that resembled a footprint, right in front of where he was kneeling. Upon closer inspection, he confirmed it. They were footprints, in the thin layer of sand that blanketed the cave's floor, leading deeper into depths of the dark cave.

Excited about his discovery, Saint Sinner held his breath, in an attempt to hear if The Boss was somewhere close-by. Twenty seconds passed, forty, then a minute. He exhaled quietly and held his breath once again, just to be sure. Nothing. Now he was certain The Boss wasn't too close by. He covered the lens of his flashlight with the palm of his hand, just to play it safe, and flipped the switch to 'on.' Slowly, carefully, he began to uncover the lens, and was able to see the nondescript environment of the cave around him. Navigating through the cave was much easier when there was light enough to see by, it turns out.

Saint Sinner continued his perilous journey, onward down the path. Each step taken was carefully placed.

He listened, smelled the air, and waited. He had been trained to make use of all his senses, and that, he did. Just as he was about to continue moving along, he cocked his head to the side, thinking he heard something in the distance.

It sounded like a soft moaning of sorts, a deep, low, vibrating moan. He didn't know what that humming, moaning sound could possibly be, but it didn't sound human at all. "There's something alien down here, something strange," he thought. He felt it more than he thought it, it seemed. Immediately, he started to silently berate himself for even entertaining the idea of something alien living in the cave. It was nonsense, and he knew it. He knew better than to jump at shadow like a teenager. Just then, he thought he had it figured out. The wind. The wind was, most likely, the cause of the moaning sound. Saint Sinner shook his head, smiling at the ridiculousness of the whole situation.

He adjusted the long-handled flashlight, in his hand, and swept the beam of light from the left to the right, slowly, inspecting every crack, gap, and shift in the sand. "Where the fuck did the old man go?" he thought, once again. The path narrowed down to the size of a sidewalk. The cave's walls rose about six meters from the floor, or close to it, and the smoothly arched ceiling continued far, out of sight.

The flashlight's beam pierced the darkness, revealing a cone-shaped slice of cavern to his already straining eyes.

The light stretched far ahead, all the way until the tunnel bottlenecked, and took a sharp turn to the right, concealing everything further from view. There had been no other branches, or forks, offering additional options for escaping, or hiding in. It was all one tunnel so far. There was nowhere else to go. The old man had to be up ahead. Perhaps he was waiting just around the corner, knowing that Saint Sinner would follow.

Pausing, Saint Sinner considered his options. He could turn away now, and leave. Just take the van, and drive away. The odds of the old bastard surviving out here, without food or water, under the blazing sun and the heat of the desert days, and the freezing nighttime temperatures, weren't very good.

Add to that the fact that he would have to walk his limping-ass sixty miles to the nearest civilization, and that virtually made his odds nonexistent. He thought about driving there, to the nearest town, and sitting there, waiting patiently in the local diner, eating cake or pie, and drinking coffee, for some ragged, shambled, form to manifest itself from the shimmering heat of the desert.

Then he could just drive his van toward the figure, point the front end at the old bastard, and put the pedal to the metal. The Boss would lay broken, and torn, defeated after an extreme struggle. A smile split Saint Sinner's face at the thought. It would be great to do, but Saint Sinner knew he would never go that route.

No, he never left things unfinished. It was against his personal code of conduct to do that. He'd wait here, slowly creep his way around the corner ahead, and hope that McCracken wasn't on the other side waiting for him, ready to blast his ass. He would fight and kill the man, just like he'd done so many times before, on other jobs, and then he'd go and collect the bounty. After that, he'd be getting ready to do it all over again. Or, maybe he'd retire. He was still young enough to start a family. He had put in his time, and made his bones. After the cash-out on this job, there really wasn't much he couldn't do. A pretty wife, two point five kids.

They could live a life of luxury for the remainder of their days.

Saint Sinner smiled that face-splitting, euphoric smile again, but it wasn't long before it was replaced by a disappointed grimace. He knew he wouldn't be doing any of those things, either. He'd keep on doing what he's always done. One day, he knew, he'd meet a challenge that he wouldn't be able to overcome, and he would die. As he lay there, dying, he'd regretfully think about how he had the chance to stop sooner, and had decided not to. He'd think about the family that he could have had, and should have, had, and then it would be all over.

Snapping back to reality, and the task at hand, he reached into his pocket and removed a few coins.

Gun ready, he whipped some of the coins around the corner, causing them to bounce, as they struck the walls and floor, and make all sorts of clinking noises and rattling pings.

Saint Sinner, listening for any sound or indication that The Boss was around, held the gun out, ready to fire. He waited, but there was nothing. He then tossed the remaining coins, and again, listened, hoping for some sort of a reaction. Still nothing.

His stomach in knots, and his heart hammering in his chest, he mentally began to prepare himself. He didn't like the situation, but he had to work with what he had. He had to see what was on the other side of that corner. He had to. Unfortunately, without a mirror, he'd have to physically check to see what laid in waiting for him. He took a deep breath, bracing himself.

He was ready to move.

A moan broke the silence.

The sound was low and deep.

It definitely wasn't the wind. It wasn't the natural sound that he'd told himself it was earlier. That strange feeling came back again, stronger than before, like there was somebody trapped between his eyes, watching him, reading his thoughts. For some reason he felt as if the presence was trying to warn him of something this time, though, his instincts hinted at impending danger.

The hair on his arms, and neck, stood on end and panic raced through him. The same feeling a young child feels, when he or she know, is absolutely sure, that there is a monster under their bed, hiding there, and waiting. A terrible monster with razor-sharp claws and needle fangs that wants nothing more than to kill.

A foreboding sense of dread washed over him, like a wave. Somewhere in the darkness, something was closing in on him, and he could feel it. He briefly looked down at the flashlight in his hand, then out at the small circle of light it cast against the wall opposite him. He shook his head, and fingered the trigger of the revolver in his other hand nervously.

He thought to himself, "Here goes nothing," and he quickly sprang from where he was standing and bolted around the corner. He was ready for action, his muscles tensed and his nerves were drawn tight, like a wire pulled to its limits and about to snap. "Motherfucker!" he said to himself, quietly, trying to keep his heart from beating out of his chest.

Saint Sinner was relieved to see the carved out passage continuing on, into a much larger, more open chamber of sorts, instead of the old prick, smiling, just as he pulled the trigger.

He aimed the flashlight all around to inspect the new area. Here was much like the rest of the tunnel, but the ceiling and floor had stalactites and stalagmites everywhere, and there was bat shit all over the place.

The large chamber, up ahead, sort of resembled the gaping maw of a hungry beast. Saint Sinner just realized something he probably should have much sooner than this. He could have kicked himself for being so careless. Here he was, shining the flashlight here, there, and everywhere with the big, open cavern still up ahead. What if The Boss was hiding in that chamber?

Nothing says "here I am" more than a beam of light, leading right back to the person dumb enough to be holding the damn thing, in a pitch-black cave. He quickly flicked off his flashlight, disappointment written all over his face, even though it was, now, too dark to be seen by anyone who could have been there. Next, he lay down flat on the ground, gun held at the ready, letting his eyes readjust to the darkness before making his way forward, crawling along the sandy stone.

In his mind, Saint Sinner figured that if McCracken was actually hiding in the antechamber, then he had a pretty good idea as to where Saint Sinner was now, thanks to the handy-dandy flashlight, and that wasn't good to think about.

The tunnel that Saint Sinner was lying in was very narrow, and relatively straight. All the Boss would have to do is stand at the end, where the tunnel actually connects to the cavern, and pop off a few shots in Saint Sinner's general direction.

There was nowhere to hide, or to take cover, and he'd more than likely end up with a few holes in him that he didn't want, need, or ask for, courtesy of that old bastard, Al. in reality, the only defense Saint Sinner really had was the darkness itself. He had hoped to avoid getting shot, the bullets passing harmlessly overhead, by crawling low to the ground and thinking outside of the box. It wasn't much, but it was all that he had, so he had to make it work.

Minutes passed and he literally inched forward. Saint Sinner estimated it must have taken him nearly half an hour to close the gap between the corner, where he started, and the entrance to the antechamber. During his time spent crawling, he had hoped to hear something that would give away the location, or even the presence, of The Boss, but the only noise he heard was that low-sounding moan, twice, and nothing else.

Without any other logical options left, he continued to make his way past the border, and into the big, open, chamber. After a few tense, quiet moments, he changed positions from prone, to a more comfortable crouch, the flashlight and pistol still at the ready.

He waited for a short while longer, allowing his heart rate to drop. Once it had, he steeled himself, said a silent prayer, and flicked his flashlight back on. The chamber was immense, much bigger than he thought it would be, he was impressed. There were several prominent ledges along the walls, for as far as the feeble light his flashlight's beam generated would allow him to see. Beyond its beam, dark shapes loomed in the shadows, more ledges, and some other cave-like adornments, no doubt.

He held his breath as the flashlight illuminated whatever he pointed it at, as it danced to the left and to the right, all around him. He could smell the dankness of the musty air, as he stayed crouched down, listening, draining his ears to listen. "What the fuck?! What the fuck was that?" he thought, his heart racing once again…

Saint Sinner, once again, killed the light, hoping it wasn't too late to save his ass. He laid all the way back down again, trying to reduce the size of the available target that he had just put out there for anyone to see.

Motionless, he held his breath and listened. A minute passed. Another. Yet another sixty seconds, or so, went by, and not so much as a peep.

He breathing and heart slowly became more normal. It was nothing he told himself. Sometimes darkness plays tricks on the mind, he knew this, it's happened to him before.

He felt comfortable to return to the crouching stance, and then he started to think, "Could the old man have, somehow, hidden himself at the cave's entrance? Was the bastard gone, did he leave just before my arrival? Or, did he flee once he heard Vino fire his gun?

If he managed to back-track to the van… He'd definitely be far, far, away from her by now, and he'd have his grimy goons on their way to come get me."

He briefly thought about his imaginary scenario he came up with earlier in the day, where he sat at the diner in the closest town eating pie, and he thought about the shoe being on the other foot, The Boss waiting for him, just to run him down, after an arduous trek across miles and miles of desert.

Being this deep in the cave, he'd never be able to hear the van's engine, or the sound of it taking off. It was a late model Ford, and ran surprisingly quiet, as it was.

He shook his head to try and rid himself of that awful idea. Now that the immediate danger had come and gone, or what he had thought was immediate danger anyway, he flicked the light back on, and ran it across the large area around him.

It was then, that the light ran across the wall that held her. The massive cave-painting could have been produced by the native cave dwellers of the area, though something about that didn't seem quite right to Saint Sinner, not at all. Even thinking about that being the situation, his stomach began to roll with the 'wrongness' of it, suggesting such a thing seemed to be a grave insult in itself.

Red, black, and white hues were spread over the stone medium, in broad strokes. The art was in some places, vague, and loose, and other, it was chillingly precise, as if it were the work of one of the latest inkjet printers, rather than a hand and archaic brushes, however long ago.

The artwork reached forty feet up, to the ceiling, and depicted what could have been Hindu gods with multiple arms, holding all manner of weapons and tools.

Added to these, were myriad other religious and mythical figures, some widely known, others obscure. All of the figures were portrayed standing in a huge circle, all surrounding on gargantuan figure in the middle of the ring. A woman of extreme, dark beauty, and perfection.

Hell, such was the extent of perfection that his unknown artist portrayed, that Saint Sinner jumped back involuntary, as his light passed over the woman, because, for a moment, he thought he was staring at a real, living and breathing, giant woman in a flowing black dress.

Her face was pale, flawless, like the surface of the moon on a clear, winter night. Her eyes were dark pools, solid, with no pupils, and a malevolent look in them, meant for any and all below her. At the edges of his vision, the shadows seemed to dance impossibly while they were under the steady light of his flashlight. But, apparently nobody informed the shadows that what they were doing was impossible, because dance, they did, giving the impression that the woman moved amid a flutter of dark robes.

Pentagrams, upside-down crucifixes, hammers, Nordic runes, stars, zodiac signs, small words written in, what looked like, every alphabet and language ever conceived, runes, Theban sigils, and more circled the powerful looking woman. Saint Sinner had a feeling that what he was looking at was very, very, old.

Potentially predating the Bronze Age, and maybe even predating man himself, although that made little sense to him.

Everything one could conjure to mind, when trying to describe the magnificence of the powerful deity, fell short. All the marks, carvings, and sigils, looked like many different hands, mediums, colors, and tools were used to create them. It was as if the work had been added to over the millennia. It was obvious that none of the work had been exclusively produced in any single era. All the evidence pointed to the opposite.

Saint Sinner shined his light across the wall again, and this time he noticed some sort of astrological-looking symbols. These weren't depictions of, say, a bull representing Taurus. This looked like a map of the stars, whole constellations were depicted in magnificent detail. This was the kind of stuff that lore spoke of. There were rings around the constellations, and what looked like expanding dimensions, making their way out and across, what Saint Sinner thought was, the universe. There was one, in particular, that reminded him of the Milky Way galaxy, great swirling strokes created a whirlpool-like design.

It also looked like the solar system, we know and love, could be seen on the outer arm of one of the swirls. Saint Sinner took his attention away from the stunning display, and looked back at the painting of the goddess.

For the first time, he noted a mark on the open palm of her right hand that almost looked like it could be a small, black pearl, or something like it. It was round, dark, and hungry looking.

The mark could have been just about anything: a doll, a ball, a marble. But, Saint Sinner didn't think any of those things were likely to be accurate. After a few moments of contemplation, the answer finally came to him. He didn't know how he knew, he just knew. It was a black hole, it had to be, and that would make sense, considering all the astrological references and drawings.

In the other hand of the goddess, she held the Earth as if it were hers, like she owned it. On the Earth, there were dotted lines that intersected at certain longitudinal and latitudinal coordinates. There was also a nautical looking compass. By the looks of it, some mathematical genius had gone ahead and mapped out important locations on the painted Earth, but what were they for?

Locations of what?

Saint Sinner rubbed his temples, while he tried to think back, to remember what it was The Boos had said earlier in the day. It didn't take him long to recall The Boss saying something about doorways, or portals to another world.

But, that was just a rumor, a myth. It had to be, right? Well, that could explain why he wasn't able to find the old man, maybe he opened a door to another world, and…. No, that was impossible. Saint Sinner disregarded the idea, dismissed it as nonsensical.

The cold, hard orbs of the goddess's eyes looked down on Saint Sinner, they held no emotion, unaffected by thousands of years spent waiting in the dark, experiencing the change from strife and conflict to elation and back again, maybe even seeing a sacrifice or two in that time, too.

With those eyes locked on him, he couldn't help but think about how new, how fresh the paint still looked after all that time spent in the dark, musty cave. It had probably been there for thousands upon thousands of years, but it looked as if it had been painted that very day.

Every time he would divert his attention elsewhere, he felt compelled, almost, to look back at her, to stare. He found it harder and harder to look away, as the shadows danced around her head, her wild, ebony strands of hair mingling with the flowing black of the robes she wore, embraced by the darkness surrounding her, the void of the universe.

A series of, what could have been runes stood out to Saint Sinner, that he hadn't noticed before, resembling the wheel of the zodiac. He started to feel as though he was being swallowed up, as he took another look at the multitude of symbols, it was all so overwhelming.

Another ancient symbol, the black sun, caught his eye. Saint Sinner recognized that black sun. He'd seen it before, but where? A book? A painting? No, it was in a series of photographs from the First World War. The black sun is set, behind the golden sun, its light invisible to the physical world. It represents the vortex, the passageway, to another dimension.

"Black holes..." he thought to himself, "even light bends to the will of such power. It's unable to resist. Entire planets and constellations are lured in, and eaten alive. Time itself stops and funnels through currents, connected to an altogether different place and time. The queen of death, goddess of the universe entire. She appeared ready to step out, into the cavern.

Saint Sinner shone his light on the floor of the cavern, right in front of the painted wall, to find an intricate black sun staring back at him. There were shallow-looking trenches that led away from the sun that were stained by something rust-colored from long, long, ago.

His gut told him that he knew what the stains most likely were, blood.

He all of a sudden felt very uneasy. "Sacrifice...To me...Centuries... Millennia... I am the demi-god, guardian of this portal...kill for me," a faint whisper.

Saint Sinner took a step back, looking over his shoulder, before he aimed the flashlight up into the face of the goddess, "What the hell was that?" he said to himself quietly, shaken by the whisper from an unknown source.

Looking up at the painting, he was awestruck all over again. He thought about how the painting was the last thing the poor sacrificed people would ever set their eyes on before the knife swiftly flashed down, ending their existence and draining their blood, watching it fill the trenches of the black sun on the ground. It was almost as if time and space had become one in this chamber, it was an odd feeling.

Speaking of odd feelings, Saint Sinner booked up into the eyes of the goddess, and for a moment, he felt like they were actually staring back into his own. Just like that, that uncanny feeling was back upon him, that same presence as before. It was an invasion of his body, his mind, and it was unsettling. It wasn't as if the presence was making demands, or anything, but he found himself walking into the center of the black sun. He felt like he was in a dream, or a trance.

That deep, low moaning sound came from every direction, all at once, it emanated from the cavern itself. For whatever reason, Saint Sinner felt, all of a sudden, compelled to lay down, grab Vino's knife, and slit his throat with a single, deep slash, letting his life blood splash down into the trenches at this feet.

He withdrew the knife, he wanted to honor himself for her, an overwhelming urge to sacrifice himself washed over him. He raised the blade, high above his head, and closed his eyes. He tensed his muscles, and was about to take the plunge, when booming laughter came from somewhere nearby, snapping Saint Sinner out of it.

He dropped the knife on the ground, shook himself violently, unbelieving what he was just about to do, and shined the flashlight all over, quickly, trying to pinpoint the source of the laughter, as the voice he'd been hearing in his head receded into the unknown, from which it came.

"Well, now, lad, you look a little woozy, if I do say so myself. It looks, to me, like you've lost your marbles. If I hadn't seen what I just saw, with my own two eyes, I never would've believed it," more throaty laughter ensued.

"What were you just doing, there, before I interrupted? Certainly, I know what it looked like you were doing, lad, but I seem to be having a hard time wrapping my head around it," The Boss's voice echoed off the walls of the chamber, making it nearly impossible to hone in on the source.

Saint Sinner, still off balance, and slightly confused, was barraged by strange visions. As if being watched through the eyes of another, he saw his own death taking place. The vision was so vivid.

There he was, kneeling in the center of the black sun on the chamber's floor, the knife held high above his head, his knuckles white from gripping the hilt. Down the knife came, in a flashing arc, from right to left slashing both his jugular and carotid artery. He could see himself topple over, to the side, lying sprawled across the floor, in a morbid semblance of one who was trying to make a snow angel, but instead of snow there was only sand and blood.

Blood that he could see himself choking on. Blood that was gushing from him, thick and crimson. It flowed from him as if it had no intention of ever stopping. His hands, chest, and stomach, were painted red by it, and the puddle grew larger beneath his body, as it worked its way outward, flowing into the trenches carved into the black sun. Saint Sinner watched on, as the light in his own eyes, the very essence of his being, grew dim and faded away to nothing, as his life drained from the gaping wound in his neck.

The experience was so real, so life-like, that Saint Sinner became overwhelmed by it all, in his panic, he clenched his fists, forgetting about the gun in his hand. "Bang! Bang! Bang! Bang! Bang! Bang!" Six shots, fired in rapid succession, uselessly hit the ground.

"Click! Click! Click!"

Again, The Boss's laughter filled the cavern, snapping Saint Sinner out of the reverie of a bad trip he seemed to be having. Too late, he had just realized what he had done. All his rounds spent, he no longer had the protection of the revolver.

Just then, The Boss stepped out from behind a mass of rocky stalagmites, no more than ten yards from where Saint Sinner had been the entire time. "Almost, lad!" he said, chuckling. "I'm surprised, shooting like that, you didn't end up catching one of those in the foot.

Now, I'm trying to make sense of this all, so bear with me, here. So, here we have a tough guy contract killer, tough as nails, always calm and collected, who apparently has lost his nerve. If I didn't know any better, I'd go as far as to say that you were afraid, scared like a wee-little girl?

And to top it off, you fire every single round at your disposal into the ground…Nobody would believe me, if I told them about his. Hell, lad, even I wouldn't believe me."

The Boss looked up at the painted deity on the cavern wall, her, in all her glory, and then set his sights back on Saint Sinner, whose eyes were already, and had been locked on him.

The Boss had his pistol pointed right at Saint Sinner, from the thirty, or so, feet away, and slowly, carefully began to walk toward him. All the thoughts, of sacrifice, and visions, of himself dying, had fled as his mind cleared up. Now, his concern was the old man with a gun who was walking toward him. But, be that as it may, Saint Sinner still had to fight the urge to look back at the painting of the goddess.

The pull that compelled him to look was strong, too strong. He-had-to-look. He shined his flashlight up the face on the wall, his mouth slightly agape. Even The Boss sneaked a quick glance at her, as he continued to walk toward him.

"Aye, she reminds me of a lass I knew back home, in Ireland. Old Miss Foley, she, too, was big and dumb looking. Had those same dark eyes, and a blank expression to match. About as smart as that, there, rock she's painted on," The Boss said, smiling. A second or two passed, passed before he continued, "After she would pleasure me, I'd slap her. Not no ordinary, run-of-the-mill slap either. I'd slap her silly, lad. Sometimes until she'd bleed. She like it too. Liked to get slapped so hard it would make her head spin, make her dizzy. There'd be handprints all over her pale, freckled skin."

Saint Sinner was hardly listening to anything The Boss was saying, he was too drawn to the painting to pay much attention or anything else. "And then, right before she'd leave, I'd walk her to the door.

Well, to the top of the stairs, anyway. I'd plant my foot in her ass and push her down them. I'd kick that wench as hard, and as fast, as I could." he laughed, "She wouldn't always fall down the stairs, though you know. Sometimes she would. Eventually, the boys began placing bets as to whether she'd fall or not. Her falling wasn't a rare occurrence, by any means," the Boss shook his head, still smiling, "she'd pick herself up off the ground, mouth full of dirt and mud, sometimes blood, and she'd still turn back around and smile at me before she started her seven-mile trek home. The boys even flavored the mud for her, sometimes. They started pissing at the foot of the stairs, "the Boss's laughter was loud, as he slapped his knee.

Saint Sinner was still being pulled toward that painting, but he managed to focus on The Boss for a moment.

"You know it rains more often than not in Ireland, and seven miles is a long way to walk in the rain, but she would do the same thing every week. She came by, letting me curse at her, and abuse her any way I'd please. Do you have any idea why that was, lad? Any at all? "The Boss asked.

Saint Sinner lowered his gaze from the goddess to meet the eyes of The Boss. "I'll tell you why... Because, to her, I was fucking god. That's why. She did what I said to do, anything at all, without question. They all did, all of them, because they knew that if they didn't, they'd have to face the wrath of this God.

I'd come down on them with a rage that would shake the very pillars of creation. The devil, himself, would be impressed, "The Boss said. He turned his attention back to the goddess of the cavern, clearly not worried about Saint Sinner making a move, or even the possibility.

"I raced further into the cave, right after I heard the shot you fired, and stumbled upon this cavern, and the paintings. At first, I thought to myself, wondering why some idiot would be in here drawing on the walls.

Obviously, it had to have been some simple fool who'd done it. I figured they probably got into a bad batch of mushrooms, or something, while they were out wandering around, picking their nose and generally making a nuisance of himself, you know, like the simple-minded fools generally do. Now, look, this moron's come and used bat shit to paint this stinking whore on the wall.

She does remind me, a lot, of my Margaret, though. Maybe I could go on up and slap her, for old time's sake what do you think about that, lad? The Boss laughed heartily, shaking his head in remembrance of the good old days. "Oh, Margaret, where has the time gone?" he seemed to say to himself.

"Looking at this abomination on the wall, the smug look on her face, like she owns the damn place, makes me sick," he said. "I've the mind to hire a crew and redecorate, paint over this pagan Mona Lisa, here, and have a likeness of me self-put up, instead." The Boss looked as though he were actually considering doing just that, then he muttered something that sounded like, "... could have been Harry Potter's mother."

Just then, another vision forced its way into the mind of Saint Sinner. This time, he saw himself wearing a flowing black robe, similar to the one worn by the goddess, standing over The Boss's wrinkly, old, naked body. He had been bound and placed at the center of the black sun, his old saggy skin hanging and covered in welts and bruises. This hand, Saint Sinner held a commercial dagger, of sorts, arm outstretched above his head.

He stood there, with the blade held high, for just a moment before he drove the blade home, with all of his strength, aiming the blade, with deadly accuracy, at the suffering old man's blackened, vicious heart.

The old man, once the most feared, infamous villain, was now little more than a pitiful, weak, shaken old fool who was about to die. The Boss opened his mouth, terror in his eyes, and pathetically screamed in protest, seeming to wither away, even before the blade had struck.

Through the dream-like vision, it tore, dragging Saint Sinner out of his murderous fancies and back to the present, to the room, to the gun pointed at him, and to his enemy who held it.

Again, the presence inside of him, that voice screamed, "Danger!"

The voice hadn't been warning him about the old man, or even about the painting, it had been trying to warn him about the sudden danger that loomed from behind him. Too late.

Slam! The stock of a gun met the back of his neck, right on the nerves that control balance and other important things like that. Saint Sinner collapsed.

He slammed the floor, his head spinning out of control. He managed to stay conscious, but he almost wished he hadn't. He was the recipient of a violent kick to the kidney, which was delivered, first class, by the Marlboro man, himself, Vasquez. Saint Sinner instantly pissed his pants, as if the "flush" button had been pressed on his bladder.

Again, the butt end of the rifle fell upon the poor Saint Sinner, but this time it hit him in the skull, and rattled his brain. Nauseating waves of pain washed over him. He could feel the warmth of his own blood flowing over his face. The third, and final blow that he happened to be awake enough to feel, brought his world from full screen, to a pinhole. He teetered on the brink, about to fall into the abyss.

Vasquez flicked on a small, battery-powered Coleman lamp. To say the little lamp was bright would be an understatement, the brilliant white light flooded the cavern with a pale, glowing luminescence. He carefully set the lamp on the floor, right beside the growing pool of Saint Sinner's blood. Vasquez began to speak, and when he did, his voice was clear and sounded fresh, like he was relaxed, he said, "So long Sinner, see you in hell." He shook his head, staring down at Saint Sinner with disappointment in his eyes, "I can't believe you didn't put a couple more holes in me, just for good measure, you know, to make sure the dead guys were really dead?" Vasquez chuckled quietly before continuing, "I know I would have had to make sure. To think you're a professional, too! He laughed at that.

"You, honestly, didn't wonder why I wasn't leading. It never even crossed your mind, really? Well, I suppose with Vino's stupid ass, which most certainly was bleeding profusely, on top of me, it would have been rather difficult to pick up on. I can understand that. I owe my life to this, here, bulletproof vest," he slapped his chest to indicate where one might wear such a vest, "and, unfortunately, for you, the mistake you made is going to cost you, and Sinner, it was mighty expensive, too."

Vasquez grinned, thinking himself clever. He towered over Saint Sinner, a pensive look about him, he said, "I was just thinking…" he reached down and picked up Vino's knife that Saint Sinner had dropped, "You and me, we're going to have some fun, buddy." He turned the knife in his hands, inspecting the blade. "I think I'm going to use this, in the name of

Vino, of course. He'd like that."

A sadistic smile slithered across Vasquez's face, as he thought about all the possibilities. He pulled a lighter from one of his pockets, flipping it between his fingers.

It took Saint Sinner a moment to realize that he had lost consciousness for some time, he looked around and tried to stand, but that was when he realized that he couldn't. He was bound, hand, and foot, and was placed in the center of the big black sun on the ground. The thought had just registered about it being light in the cavern, and not only that, but Vasquez appeared to be alive, well, and standing beside him with a lighter. "Not good, not good at all," he thought.

A flicking noise could be heard, as the lighter lit up, a small flame danced around and cast faint shadows as it moved closer.

A shooting, stinging pain flared up through his leg as the flame touched his skin, instantly bubbling up the flesh. The smell of scorched hair and skin assaulted his nose.

Saint Sinner struggled and fought, twisting, and turning every-which-way, trying desperately to loosen, slip, or break his restraints before the pain broke him. He struggled and fought in vain. Apparently, Lady Luck was on her lunch break. The smell was terrible, and it grew stronger still, reminding him of active duty. Reminding him of the aftermath of a terrorist attack, the bodies pulled from the rubble of a building that had been bombed, broken, missing limbs, charred, blackened, and skin. It was the smell of death.

Saint Sinner had to do something. He had to find a way to stop the pain. He bit down on his lip, hard, trying to distract himself from the hellish pain he was experiencing at the hands of Vasquez.

He thought he might be able to focus on the pain in his lip, in order to focus less on the fact that he was slowly being burned alive. No matter what happened, though, no matter what these two son-of-bitches decided to put him through, he decided that would-not-be giving them the satisfaction of hearing him scream out in pain.

"You see, lad, crime does pay," The Boss said, smiling and watching from a distance, "and in the end, the bad guys do win. Always have. Always will."

Vasquez cocked his head, his eyes lowering to Saint Sinner's feet, as he brought the flame from one, already toasted, toe to another. The all-to-familiar sizzle and flare sent another excruciating wave of pain through Saint Sinner. A blister popped, just like a child poking a bubble, and a clear liquid seeped from the wound. The liquid flashed when it hit the flame, like water hitting a grease-covered skillet.

Sweat poured from Saint Sinner's forehead, as the pain became more and more intense. Vasquez was cooking him alive, one inch at a time, with his red Bic lighter.

The Boss, standing still as a statue, was watching the expression on Saint Sinner's face, as blood started to trickle down his chin from his teeth biting into, and through, his lip. Still, he refused to scream.

Every muscle ached, every nerve in his body seemed to be screaming for him. His body flipped, spun, tossed, and turned in his struggle to not scream out.

This experience was, by far, the worse pain he had ever felt. He was both surprised and disappointed that he hadn't passed out yet. The torturous waves kept rolling through him, vast, deep, and bitter cold.

Vasquez worked his way across all ten of his toes before moving on to the soft, sensitive flesh on Saint Sinner's calf muscle. He let the flame flicker his knee cap, on the backside, where the soft fold of skin burning brought a whole new meaning to the word pain.

Saint Sinner managed to pry his eyes open and look up at the goddess on the wall. She had those ebony eyes that were cruel, menacing, and all-knowing. They seemed to be peering back at him, into his very soul. He held her gaze without blinking, as sweat dropped off his face and onto the floor. His hands, thrashed open and closed, and his legs pumped back and forth.

He was in agony.

He was forced to use all his willpower, everything he had learned over the years, to not scream out. He shook sweat, spit, and blood from his face, but still he managed to focus on those two bottomless, black pools.

In his mind he called out to her, a desperate, angry outburst, and "Do you like what you see? Are you happy, now?! Here is your pound of flesh, your sacrifice! I am yours, here, now, in this God-forsaken cave, forgotten by time! I die for you! My pain is all for you! I scream not for my enemy, but for you, alone! It's all for you! and for what?

 What, for my sacrifice?

For my strength, my devotion?

 What, in return?"

Saint Sinner was delirious with pain, as Vasquez decided to change things up, to keep things interesting. He started to say something, no doubt, meant to strike fear into the heart of Saint Sinner, but it had no effect.

Saint Sinner was too far gone to be listening to him ramble. He didn't hear a word of it. Nor did he notice as the first slice of skin was flayed from his shin.

Vasquez grabbed ahold of the strip of skin that had been sliced by Vino's knife, with a leather man's pliers, and literally tore the flesh from Saint Sinner's bones. Vasquez worked its way around one leg, and then went to work on the other. All the while, Saint Sinner locked eyes with the goddess on the wall, her eyes held his gaze.

The Boss took a seat, smiling serenely, clearly enjoying the show. Saint Sinner's head was pinned against the ancient floor, fixed in position, looking up at the queen of darkness above him. Something looked different about the paint, it looked wet, freshly coated.

There were spots that dripped downward in rivulets. Her face seemed even more flawless than before, beautiful, perfect.

Now, Saint Sinner was hovering in the air, above his own body, looking down at it. He no longer felt the feeble attempts of Vasquez. The Boss got up and walked over. He stood right next to Saint Sinner's head.

He leaned down, and he followed his line of sight.

He sneered, and glared at the goddess on the wall before looking back at Saint Sinner, "I see what you're doing, lad. I have to admit, as much as I hate your fucking guts, I have to admire a man that can focus enough to withstand this kind of pain. It's impressive. You've cheated me out of my fun, lad, by inducing this half-assed, hippy trance upon yourself." He shook his head, frowning.

"So, you lock eyes with the whore on the wall, and everything is okay? Is that how it works?"

"What did you do, offer yourself to her for help, or something?"

"Is she helping you, lad?" the Boss glanced at her once again, and in one fluid motion, pulled out his revolver.

"Did she speak to you, tell you everything was going to be okay? Tell you that we'll be letting you go at the end? Did she, now, lad?" the Boss glanced, a second time, up at the wall, this time he looked her dead in the eyes before turning his attention back on Saint Sinner, "Well, lad, if she told you all that nonsense, she damn-well lied to you," he laughed a cruel laugh.

"It'll be just the opposite, for you.

Death is all that you have to look forward to now, and there be nothing your painted friend can do to stop it. This is MY will, what I command is law! I am god, here!"

The Boss swung his arm up and shot two rounds into the piece of goddess on the wall. Vasquez jumped up, grinning.

"I am the giver of life and the bringer of death! I have the final say as to whether you live or die, lad. She can look at you all she wants, and you her, but I say nothing will come of it!"

The Boss raised his arm, once again, he pointed his gun right at Saint Sinner, point-blank. The Boss quickly angled the gun away from Saint Sinner and popped off three more shots, the blasts echoing off the walls, and the bullets ricocheting into the shadows.

"I don't have much time, lad. I've got to go. For, I have castles to conquer and kings to kill. This is where your time on Earth comes to an end.

You will know, here and now, in this shit-hole cave that and the whore on the wall is nothing more than that, a whore on a wall.

"She is no goddess!" he said.

"She is nothing but a peyote-induced cave painting. She couldn't stop me from farting, let alone stop me from killing you," The Boss laughed maniacally, "there is only one God, here!" he glared at Saint Sinner, as he continued to play out the last words. He aimed his pistol at Saint Sinner's head, "... and that mother fucking God is ME!"

The Boss winked and pulled the trigger. The blast tore through Saint Sinner's left eye, exploding the socket, and mutilating the brain behind it. Saint Sinner's world had come to an end, and he was grateful for it.

All life had left Shamus Quinn, once known as Saint Sinner, the spotless military career, the contract killing, his entire being had been exhaled into the ancient cave, under the close supervision of Helena, queen of the dead and gate keeper of time and space. She was the spirit of the void, the black hole connecting our galaxy to the universe. The Boss had entered her sanctuary and defiled her name, denounced her power.

He had attempted to sacrifice in his own name on the hallowed, sacred ground that belonged to her. His temerity had awoken her from her eternal slumber.

She was awake and angry. She took away his power, watched him leave, and set forth a balancing force.

Blackness.

Saint Sinner knew blackness.

He was conscious and aware of it without feeling the need for his body. There was no breath, no pulse, and no blood coursing through his veins.

He remembered.

He had been sacrificed, left on the floor of the ancient cave. He remembered all the symbols. He remembered her eyes. Death had its advantages. Rest, plenty of time for rest. Awareness.

How was it possible?

Awareness of self, without self?

He was considering this, when he saw movement. A small pinprick of white. A dot, it was growing, and it glowed like a distant star. It grew to the size of a headlight, then he was able to see more.

Black, flowing, and swirling though out the whiteness. Robes. Hair. Arms. Eyes.

Time and space seemed to be carrying her, moving her along. Closer, now, she had come off the wall and stood before him. Speaking thoughts into his awareness. Black eyes, and lips the color of dead roses, the only one that mattered.

Her voice was not sound, but earthquakes of vibration, the whispers of the Earth. She breathed him back into existence. Into his body.

"I am Hel, the goddess of death, born of Loki and Angerboda. I hail from Helheim, under a root of the World Tree, Yggdrasil. I am Mimir's twin sister, evolved from the ancient race of giants. I am the guardian of sacred, mystic treasure. A being of supreme power, given knowledge by Wotan, I am the guardian of the door to the nine realms. I give your life renewed.

Death, without my blessing, means nothing.

He can no more force it than he could grow wings and fly. Such things are not for those like him. Seek revenge upon him and his. Bathe in their blood, drink your fill, and glut yourself from their crushed skulls. Only when my throat is quenched, shall you be set free. Rise, guest, for I grant your life with my kiss of death."

A kiss, she blew from her lips, and out came the breath of life, from death. "You are my reaper. Vengeance is your new mission. Go forth!" Saint Sinner sat up, drawing in a deep, gasping, breath, his first, since his last, thirteen minutes prior. He found himself comfortable in the surrounding darkness and silence, the musty, dank smell of deep-earth all around him. Seeing things through his left eye was different.

He could see things in tints of red, like he was looking through a filter, and darkness, apparently, meant nothing. He knew it was dark, yet he could see a rat nibbling on a piece of his discarded flesh.

All of a sudden, he was more parched than he had ever been.

He needed a drink, and he needed one, now. Instinct welled up inside of him, too fast to stop, he snatched the unsuspecting rodent up, snapped its neck with a twist, and tore its head clear off.

Next thing he knew, he held the lifeless body of the rat upside down, above his lips, drinking its blood. As the blood entered Saint Sinner's body, a vision flashed through his mind, gone almost before it began.

It was The Boss walking, followed by Vasquez. They hopped into the white van and drove away, without a second look back. They didn't even pay vino's corpse any mind before leaving. Saint Sinner's legs, fresh from death, were healed. Scarred over. The gruesome wounds that had been afflicted, had all been marked out in darkness, the blackest-looking ink imaginable. The same black as the color of her eyes. The tattoos marking the sites of his torturous treatment, were the only evidence of the deadly acts that had taken his life.

Saint Sinner ran his hand over the scar where his left eye had been. The smooth skin, covering the socket, provided no hindrance to his newly gained sight. He retained normal vision in his right eye. Looking through his left eye was like looking at sun with your eyes closed. Flexing his limbs, he felt stronger that he had ever been. He walked out of the cave and saw night came alive in every direction. The desert air was cooler, and more welcoming than he could remember.

Bright, and full, was the moon, surrounded by a breathtaking blanket of stars. Saint Sinner looked longingly at the entrance to the cave.

Faintly, he could hear the song of the goddess. Ancient was he worship. He wasn't afraid. He knew she held him in the palm of her hand.

He nodded to her before walking over to where the fresh tire tracks in the sand led off toward the distant lights. He followed with his eyes, then with his feet.

With his first step, he knew what he intended to do.

It was what he was good at.

She knew it too and pulled the strings to his body with laughter.

He would kill, against his will.

She would never stop.

Did he have a choice?

To be continued...

SAINT SINNER
Life from the kiss of death

SCOTT NIEMIC

COPYRIGHT 2018

Smashwords edition

"This is far enough, lads.

Kill the engine, and haul this soon-to-be-dead man out of my van.

And remind him to mind his manners," a cheery voice said from the front seat.

Saint Sinner did his best to get his bearings. His head was woozy, like the day after a long night of drinking. In fact, it wasn't the drinking that caused his blackout. It was presumably what somebody had slipped into his drink that was the problem. Whatever it was, it hit him hard and took him down like a tranquilizer dart takes down a rhino.

His memory was foggy at best.

His recollection of the prior night was fragmented, bits and pieces coming together to form a distorted image. Something about a white van, but what about it?

He thought there was something odd about the white van. Something about it was off and seemed out of place. The more he thought about it, the more things began to fall in place. It still felt as if he was viewing the events of the previous night through a thick haze. He vaguely remembered seeing two strange men near the white van, painting a neighbor's fence. There was something about those two guys, too.

He didn't know what, but for some reason they were just as out of place as the van was. What was it though? He just couldn't seem to put his finger on it, so he'd ignored the nagging feeling he had in his gut that told him something wasn't right.

After all, what was so strange about a couple butt-ugly guys working, painting his neighbor's... Just then he remembered what it was that struck him as odd about those two "painters."

Thinking back, as best he could granted the grogginess, aside from the fact that these guys didn't much look the part of your typical, everyday painters, he remembered seeing drops of paint all over the sidewalk. No professional painting company would be careless enough, sloppy enough to make a mess of the public sidewalk. With times being as tough as they've been, and the economy being shit, that would be reason enough for businesses to be on point. There was simply no room for carelessness.

That, right there, was a red flag. Ordinarily, he would have picked up on something like that. But, after the last few exhausting days of navigating back streets, exploring shady places, meeting unsavory people, and fulfilling his contractual obligations by eliminating predetermined targets, he was spent.

He was taxed, both physically and mentally, so much that his guard slipped, and he headed to a bar for a much deserved drink, despite the fact that he had quit drinking. Twice. In the past month. Never mind that, though, it was his birthday.

Friday the thirteenth.

Forty years had passed since his teen-aged mother had given him up to the Commonwealth of Massachusetts.

In his line of work, to live past thirty would be a blessing. The situation seemed to call for a celebration, so why not one for the road? This one, last time, for real. No bullshit. That's what he told himself, right before he headed over and walked into the Erie Pub, one of Boston's oldest Irish taverns.

That night the bartender had sent him a free drink, which he accepted. It was totally out of character for him to do so, but it was his birthday, and somebody did pay for the round. That was mistake number two. About three shots of Jamison later, he paid his tab at the bar before he left.

He hiked over to the intersection of Ashmont and Adams, to a mini-mart liquor store that was owned by a Greek family. The deli in back of the mini-mart was one of Dorchester's best-kept secrets. The drinking had made him hungry, so he ordered a steak bomb sub and an ice tea Snapple to go. Mistake number three. He never ate out. Being out in public was asking for trouble, an unnecessary risk, for somebody in his line of work. But, it was his birthday, right?

It wasn't like he had spent the entire night at the Glass Slipper, watching the girls up on the stage shaking their "money makers" or anything. Although, that didn't exactly sound like a terrible time, either. Maybe for his birthday next year.

He began to devour his sub. He took a swig of his Snapple and looked at the back of the cap so he could read the Snapple fact.

In the back of his mind he thought about where he might choose to live next, after this place. Just then, his legs began to feel weak, shaky. The Snapple fact may as well have been written in Chinese at this point, because there was no way in hell he could read what it said with his vision as blurry as it had become.

Everything faded to black around him. He felt like he was falling. Falling... That was the last thing he could remember. In retrospect, he had broken the golden rule: never expose yourself for too long but, he was a hard worker, and some jobs took more time than others to complete.

Regardless of however long it would take, he would never leave a job unfinished. Growing up, hard work, downing pints of Guinness, and taking pride in one's work was instilled into the young Shamus McGregor. He was proud of where he came from and never hesitated to lend a helping hand when needed. He was your typical, good-hearted Irish boy from the Boston area.

Snapple... it had to have been the Snapple.

Or maybe that steak bomb?

No, it was definitely the God-damned Snapple. As he sat, replaying the night's events, scene by scene, it suddenly struck him. Most, if not all, products come with a tamper-evident seal on them to let the consumer know whether the product has been opened or not.

For the life of him, he couldn't recall hearing the signature popping sound when he opened that damn Snapple. He remembered noticing at the time, but he shrugged it off and drank the refreshing beverage anyway. That had to be it. This was the kind of thing that led to him giving up drinking in the first place. Nothing stronger than lemonade, he had vowed. Yet, here he was again in the same predicament.

Getting sloppy and missing important details.

He had decided that when knocking off accountants, bodyguards, and under-bosses, he really couldn't afford to be sloppy anymore. It turns out, when you start taking people like that, people who belong to world-wide, notorious crime syndicates out, it doesn't take very long for the bigger fish, the guys at the top of the hierarchy, to take notice.

People like that don't appreciate it when their people start dying. In fact, people like that tend to get pissed off when things like that start happening. As a result, people like that tend to do crazy things in order to get their people to stop being killed off. Things like offering a ten million dollar reward, payable to anyone, for whoever is able to put a stop to the problem. In this case, Saint Sinner happened to be the problem. Whose problem, you ask?

Remember the cheery-voiced, older gentleman, with the Irish accent, who was seated in the front of the van? Bingo. He had personally offered the ten million dollar contract. Saint Sinner was sure of it.

So, it all came down to this... Killer's killing killers. Who was right, who was wrong? Good, bad? Which side was righteous, which was hell-bent?

That is the million dollar question.

The way Saint Sinner looked at it, there were two kinds of people in the world: Bad and Evil. Shoplifters, drug users/dealers, and the white-collar criminals, the fraudsters and immoral accountants who supplemented their bank accounts with illegally-acquired funds and those who fudged numbers and added a few extra zeroes to the end of their bank account totals: bad people, but not evil.

Ex-military snipers, recruited secretly and sworn to secrecy, hired for "shadow ops" and taking out targets around the world in the name of counter-terrorism and preventative maintenance. In other words, murder-for-hire. Hired by the alleged "good guys," though. Again, bad, not evil, right? Bad guys hired to do good, or good guys who are justified in being bad?

Hard to tell. Evil people, on the other hand, didn't care about the money, or whether what they did was for a good reason or not. It had nothing to do with the difference between right and wrong for them. Saint Sinner viewed evil as a sickness that people either had, or didn't have.

Saint Sinner was a bad guy, who made a living killing evil men. Evil men who harbored dark secrets. Some of the things these guys had done would put your modern-day horror movie to shame in comparison. We're talking about some real pieces of work here. These guys were comparable to Silence of the Lambs, as far as gruesomeness, but they lacked the same element of intelligence and psychological aptitude that kept people interested.

Basically these guys were known to torture their victims in cruel and unusual ways. Some of them at their very own twisted torture chambers located in the dungeon like basements of the private estates. Evil men, the heads of their corrupt empires whose goals are all the same: unlimited wealth and global domination. Evil men, not like Saint Sinner.

Not like most people.

Evil men.

Not only were these guys the cream of the crop but they also managed to make their way onto America's shit-list. It's no secret things need to be taken care of sometimes, and when that time comes, who do you call?

Someone like Saint Sinner, that's who. He is one of the best in the field, and he comes highly recommended.

His specialty is taking out politically sensitive targets who are connected to terrorists or terrorism, in one way or another. This is exactly why he currently found himself coming-to, bound in the back of the white van that belonged to those bullshit-painters that had struck him as being out of place in the first place, the night before. The voice in his head was loud, and it sounded like a disappointed parent when it said, "See what happens when we drink?"

They probably had been conducting surveillance and had an eye on him, since his Gulfstream touched down at Logan Airport. They were probably the type that had in-depth files on their targets.

Files that included everything you could think of, including your server's account of what you had ordered for dinner at the restaurant you went out to eat at the night before. Everything. These guys had most likely been watching, been waiting, and been planning exactly how they were going to intercept Saint Sinner for a while now. Probably even before he had left for L.A., a month prior, to handle the last contract he had accepted.

A kiddie-porn distributor. This guy was also linked to laundering money in Southeast Asia with representatives from notorious crime syndicates. Mr. Sotto was his name, and he was the recipient of one well-placed, high-velocity fifty-caliber round that was delivered, first-class, right to his dome.

After receiving the package, there wasn't much left of the guy from the chin up. It'll be a closed casket funeral for Mr. Sotto. That was just one evil man scratched off the never-ending list of shit-bags that needed to be dealt with.

There are so many that need to be handled, that when choosing a contract, you had to be selective and very particular. You want to choose a target that matters. Every hit needs to count. A good target is somebody that when taken out, will make waves in the water.

Someone that plays a key part in the grand scheme of things. Somebody, when removed, who will cause a void in the system. Someone the big guy at the top of the pyramid is going to hear about and be furious about losing. But, never mind all that. The point is, these guys were professionals. Once the drugs kicked in, it was a wrap. Down for the count and into the van.

There was only one man in the Western Hemisphere that wanted him bad enough and had the resources to accomplish a feat such as this. Surveillance. The hired goons, posing as painters. Simply being able to know the target well enough to successfully spike a beverage with drugs, with the fore-knowledge allowing for the right beverage to be chosen, and on top of that, having the target consume that very same, drugged beverage. All-in-all, it was rather impressive to think about. It was a perfectly executed plan. Had they wanted him dead on the spot, they very well could have killed him. The fact that he was still alive meant only one thing. They must have plans for Saint Sinner, something special in mind pertaining to how he's to be disposed of. But, for now, he was alive, and as far as he was concerned, that was a mistake on their part. Being blindfolded, gagged, and bound, there wasn't much he could do, but he was able to think about what he might do, if given the opportunity, so that's what he did.

Suddenly, the van skid to a halt.

He could hear dirt and small pebbles being kicked up and hitting the undercarriage of the van, as it came to a stop. Somebody killed the engine. Heart pounding, Saint Sinner was in survival mode. The years of rigorous training had instilled in him a sense of clarity, nerves of steel.

He took a deep breath and cleared his head as best he could. "Pull yourself together, this is it. No second chances here. Nobody is going to save you, but yourself," he thought. Just then, he heard a loud creaking sound as the doors in the rear of the van were opened behind him. Immediately, hellish-heat filled the air around him, hot and dry. Using the limited clues he had available, he desperately tried to determine where he might be. He definitely wasn't in Boston anymore, the heat and dusty, dry air told him that much. He had to be somewhere in the South. Or, maybe in the West. Thinking like that only led him to more questions, though.

How long was he out for?

One day?

Two?

A week?

Before he was able to come to a conclusion, the smell of cigarette smoke filled the air and distracted him from his train of thought. What seemed like a second later, he was being dragged from the back of the van by what appeared to be, two men with the combined strength of a bull and an iron grip.

Out of the van by what appeared to be, two men with the combined strength of a bull and an iron grip. Out of the van and on his own two feet, he heard someone say, "Vino?" and another man reply, "Yeah, boss?" the elderly man with the Irish accent was apparently the boss, and this Vino guy an underling. No doubt, he was one of the two guys who dragged Saint Sinner from the van.

"Please remove the blindfold and take the gag out of our friend's mouth. We're not uncivilized, now, are we lad?" the boss said. "No sir, not at all, boss," Vino said, his voice scratchy, grating. "But Vino, do be sure our friend here, understands just how important good manners are to me. Vasquez will assist you. Make sure things are made clear, and I mean crystal." Vino and Vasquez both replied, "Sure thing, boss" and "Yes, sir."

Saint Sinner, still as blind as a bat due to the hood that had promptly been pulled over his head at some point during his abduction, was still fully capable of hearing what had been transpiring around him.

He had been listening to the conversation between his captors the entire time, hanging on every word as if his very life depended upon it. He knew the blow was coming, but from which direction and where it would land was still a mystery to him. He tensed his muscles in preparation, but wasn't expecting what felt like a knee to the stomach.

It was a hard hit, and it knocked the wind out of him. Saint Sinner doubled over in pain, gasping, trying to catch his breath. The two henchmen got him back on his feet, standing him up straight. For a second, he was brought back in time. Flashbacks from a previous job in Iraq of all places, flooded his memory.

He remembered himself using the same exact methods, the same tactics, using fear to motivate his targets to cooperate. Being temporarily blinded adds a whole new element of fear to the equation. Sometimes the uncertainty, not knowing, makes things worse. Far worse. Tactics like these, yield results.

Saint Sinner was pulled from his not-so-pleasant, trip down Memory Lane by the sound of Vino's scratchy voice, "Let that be a reminder to you. Mind your manners, tough guy. I don't think you'll forget, but just in case..."

To Saint Sinner's left, he could hear fast paced, shuffling footsteps approaching. The footsteps stopped a second later, right next to where he stood, and in the blink of an eye, pain blossomed in his lower back. It felt as though he had been kicked hard by somebody wearing some sort of pointed boots. Cowboy boots, perhaps. Down, like a sack of potatoes, he went. That had to have been a kidney shot. He'd most likely be pissing blood for a week, if he even lived that long.

He let out a muffled grunt as he hit the ground, but refused to give them the satisfaction of hearing him cry out. He would not scream, even if he could, or beg them for mercy. That wasn't his style. He was a tough son-of-a-bitch, who knew he could take pain just as easily as he could give it. He could hear one, if not both, of the cronies chuckling as they picked him up off the ground for the second time.

Saint Sinner didn't know exactly what these guys had in mind, or in store for him, but he had the sudden feeling that it was going to be a long night. He knew that if their plan was to simply kill him, then it wouldn't be so simple after all. He knew they'd most likely drag it out and take pleasure in making him suffer.

Saint Sinner knew one thing for certain, and two things for sure. They most certainly didn't bring him all the way out here for a picnic.

If, for some reason these clowns didn't finish the job, and left him alive, he would be back with a vengeance, and would make it a point to personally execute each and every one of them.

Slowly, very slowly.

And, if these guys were incompetent enough to allow him to somehow escape, again he would be back with a vengeance, and he would make it a point to execute each and every one of them, just as slowly. But, in his heart, he knew that these guys had no intention of letting him live. Had they simply wanted to send a message, they could have used the damn telephone...

In Saint Sinner's world, the transition from night to day was instant. Blinding darkness was replaced by blinding white light, as the hood that had been pulled over his head, for however long it had been there, was removed. The sun's light was so bright, it was staggering. His eyes began to water profusely as they struggled to adjust to the illuminated environment.

Bathed in the bright light, it took him a few agonizing moments to be able to finally see, but it didn't take him long at all to feel the barrel of the gun that had been pressed against his back, right between his shoulder blades. At about the same time, Vino said, "No funny stuff, tough guy, you understand me?"

Finally Saint Sinner was able to put a face to this "Vino" with the grating voice that he'd been listening to. The two men locked eyes for a moment, each man sizing the other up. It may have only been a quick meeting of the eyes, but in that moment Saint Sinner seemed to be peering into the very soul of Vino. The intensity of the stare, the now hatred that was passed from his eyes and into the very being of the other man, made Vino feel very uncomfortable. Inferior even. Vino blinked once, then twice, trying to get the attention off of himself. The moment had passed, it was over. Saint Sinner now saw what he was looking for: weakness.

Based on his recently garnered information, his mind began to race to formulate some sort of plan that would enable him to take advantage of Vino's lack of self-confidence and mental prowess and ultimately save his own life in the process. Although Vino did have the gun that was pressed tightly against his back, and he most certainly would be nervous and unstable enough to pull the trigger at the slightest of provocations, so that put Saint Sinner in a very precarious predicament. It was a fine line, and he would have to walk it very carefully, if he didn't want to end up with anymore holes in him than he already had. Which, of course, he didn't.

Vino flashed a crooked grin, full of yellow, half-rotten teeth, and he grabbed ahold of the corner of the duct tape that had been placed over Saint Sinner's mouth, to keep the gag in place. He began to slowly, ever so slowly, peel back the tape. It must have hurt, being removed so slowly like that, but then again, that was the point. Vino seemed to be getting impatient though, and ripped it the rest of the way off.

Naturally, some of the skin stuck to the duct tape, and when he yanked it hard, like he did, some of the skin came off with the tape. Saint Sinner winced as the tape came off. He spat the gag out immediately and licked his lips, where the tape had been. He tasted blood. The gag hit the ground with a soft thudding noise and kicked up a little dust as it landed. He shook his head and spit a few times, to get the taste of blood out of his mouth, before looking out towards the horizon.

Waves of heat rose from the sand that had been sitting, cooking, all day in the blazing sun, and distorted things far-off in the distance.

Things seemed to shimmer, and it almost looked as though there might be an oasis, a refreshing pool of water, among the dunes. Saint Sinner knew better than that, though, it was a mirage, and he knew it. As soon as his eyes had adjusted, and he was able to see, he could tell he was in the middle of a desert. Which desert, though, he had no idea.

Just then he tried to bring one of his hands up, to shield his eyes from the brilliance of the sun, and at the same time to give himself a better view of things around him, but he had forgotten that his hands were bound by heavy-duty, industrial zip-ties. Needless to say, his hands weren't going anywhere.

He had to find a way out of these restraints. If he couldn't do that, he wasn't getting anything else done, and that meant he was as good as dead.

He started to do what he was able to do.

It wasn't much, but it was better than nothing and better than simply waiting around to die.

He started looking around for landmarks he'd be able to remember, in the event he was able to escape. He took in his entire situation, using any and everything at his disposal to gain an upper-hand. After he did a quick, mental recon, and all things were considered, two words came to mind-All bad.

Based on what he saw when he looked around, the acrid, desolate landscape, he knew that he had been taken somewhere far away, to a desert, most likely somewhere in the Southwest United States or in Mexico. The first place that came to mind was the Chihuahua

Desert.

One hundred fort thousand square miles of nothing but sand and the occasional cactus. A true desert wasteland that spanned from Arizona, all the way through to the end of Texas and into the heart of Mexico, the land of the lawless, where the men were quick to kill and the women were even more so.

Things started to make sense, all of a sudden. The Mexican badlands would be a perfect place to bring somebody like Saint Sinner, somebody who needed to be disposed of. No worries, when it came to disposing of the body. No worries about civilians accidentally coming across the remains, not out here. No worries about having to deal with the authorities. A perfect place, indeed.

Saint Sinner took note of the single-lane, horse-trail-looking road that trailed off into the distance. It had to have been made for horses, or for donkeys, because it most certainly wasn't wide enough for two vehicles to pass side-by-side. And, judging by the looks of the trail, it wasn't frequented by vehicles at all. This furthered his belief that he had been brought into Mexico.

The heat was scorching, it had to have been well over one-hundred degrees in the sun. The sweat beaded on his forehead and slowly dripped down his face and off his chin. He was half-surprised to find that his sweat didn't evaporate before hitting the ground. In sweltering heat like this, it felt as though it might.

Everything about the environment, where Sinner found himself currently, was harsh and unforgiving. It was fortunate, for him, that he had been through rigorous training that included climate-based survival.

He was relatively experienced, when it came to being exposed to extreme environments. Being left in the desert, to fend for himself, wouldn't kill him. But, being left in the desert, to fend for himself with a bullet in his back could definitely be a problem.

As if to emphasize the point, Vino pushed the barrel of his gun a little further into Saint Sinner's spine. The gesture brought him back to his predicament, out of his mind and into the present. Just then, another man stepped out from the far-side of the van. He had been there the entire time, waiting and listening.

The guy was a giant, he was massive. He had to have been pushing damn-near seven feet tall. He looked like he could have made the cut the N.B.A.

Not only was he tall, but he had a chiseled physique. His walnut-colored skin looked worn, or weathered, but it was stretched tight across his muscular bulk. He was toned, cut, even. This man was in excellent shape.

He wore a western-styled hat, the ones you'd see country singer's wearing in their music videos, on his head and a button down shirt, blue, with a plaid pattern. He had straight-legged jeans on, and a belt with an over-sized buckle. Sure-as-shit, on his feet were cowboy boots. Now Saint Sinner knew where that kick had come from, he had been wondering about that...

"Vasquez," he thought, narrowing his eyes at the man.

Vasquez had cold, hard eyes, and a mean stare. The eyes of a killer, seasoned in the field. Saint Sinner had seen countless others with the same look in their eyes. He had killed countless others with the same look in their eyes as well.

He wasn't afraid of Vasquez, but he was wary. Men like him are dangerous, and Saint Sinner knew better than to disregard, or worse underestimate, a man like Vasquez. Being over-confident, to the point of being borderline careless, has been the cause of death to many a good man. As far as Saint Sinner was concerned, you could never be too careful. He wasn't trying to be the next fatality due to lack of attention to detail.

Vasquez looked vaguely familiar to him, but he couldn't place where he might have seen him before. Surely, he would have been able to recognize someone of that stature, had he seen him before. At least, he thought he would have, anyway.

The process of scouring his memory, in order to discover where, or when, it might have been that he had seen Vasquez before, was interrupted when another, third man stepped into Saint Sinner's line of sight. He could hardly believe his eyes. At first glance, anybody would have seen the grandfatherly, older gentleman wearing a white baseball hat and expensive-looking track suit, and thought nothing of it. But, that was just a façade, and Saint Sinner knew it.

Standing before him was a criminal mastermind, a living legend. This man was somebody important. Important enough to have the attention of mafias and cartels, alike. The man led the largest, and most notorious, crime syndicates in the North American continent.

A ruthless killer that started at the bottom and clawed his way to the top, using dead bodies as stepping stones on the path to power. He was infamous, a king of the underworld. He was a very thorough man, and preferred to handle certain jobs himself. If he was here, it meant bad news. Saint Sinner knew who he was, not by name of course, nobody knew his name, but by looks. He had only seen pictures of the man before.

People referred to him simply as "The Boss," and his reputation preceded him, wherever he went.

For a moment, only the whistling of the wind could be heard, as the Boss stood, staring at Saint Sinner. The wind was refreshing while it lasted, but it was gone just as suddenly.as it appeared. Instantly, the oppressive heat washed back over the group of men like a wave, a wave of discomfort.

Movement, in the periphery of his vision, caught his attention. He looked, for a split second, without turning his head, and saw it was nothing more than a tumbleweed that had caught on the short breeze and came to a halt, along with the wind that had propelled it. Without saying a word, the Boss looked off in the direction of the setting sun.

There was angry sort-of beauty in the sunset as it fell from the sky and, in its failing light, painted the world myriad shades of reds and oranges. There was nothing quite like it, especially here, in the desert.

Saint Sinner's mind started to wander. He couldn't help himself from thinking strange thoughts. Thoughts of the ancient civilizations, the Aztecs, Incas, and Mayas. Thoughts of human sacrifice crossed his mind. He found himself as being the human sacrifice, his death meant to alleviate the anger of the divine being. He shook his head, clearing his thoughts. It must be dehydration finally kicking in. He was rather parched. Clearly, his mind wasn't as sharp as usual. Not good.

The Boss stood, one hand in his pocket, and the other holding what had to be the most exotic-looking Desert Eagle that Saint Sinner had ever seen. This gun was a work of art. Not only was it silver plated, but it had a gold inlay, as well.

The handle too, was funny. It was crafted from fine ivory, no doubt it was carved from a very expensive, most likely illegally-attained, elephant tusk that had been imported from somewhere in Africa for an obscene amount of money. That was definitely the man's style.

The gun and the outfit made a very odd combination. Saint Sinner could see how, based on how the guy looked, it would be very easy to underestimate him, and he was sure that people had made the mistake many times while he ascended to the top of the food chain. Here he was, seventy-two years old, living like he's still in his prime, enjoying life and having fun, but still as deadly an adversary as ever.

Just as Saint Sinner had been lost in thought a moment ago, The Boss seemed to be lost in thought now. He was scanning the horizon, a serene smile on his face.

It was as if he had been taken by the beauty of the scene. It looked like, if he could have taken a picture, or better yet painted one.

Saint Sinner didn't know which was more disturbing, the look of rapture on The Boss's face, or the gun pointed at his own.

Al "the Boss" McCracken, wasn't your run of the mill criminal. If you put together a visualization, a tree-chart, of the hierarchy of global organized crime, you'd find The Boss at the pinnacle.

He's known as an apex predator, top dog, and feared by any and everyone who knew who, or what, he was. Rightfully so, too. He commanded the top players in North America as well as Western Europe. Some of the most notorious, organized killers, cut-throats, and contract thugs the world had ever known, with an iron-fist, no less, but anybody who was stupid enough to laugh at the absurd irony of the situation was taken care of, already long dead.

The Boss hadn't simply been handed his position, either. According to the rather thick file Saint Sinner had on the patriarch, he had risen to power the old-fashioned way. Like many others, he started living the life during childhood.

At a young age, he had already made quite a name for himself, as he quickly climbed his way through the ranks of his neighborhood street gang, back in Dublin.

He started out small, with menial jobs like running numbers for local bookies and miscellaneous side jobs. Of all the work he had been assigned, collecting debts was his favorite. Not only did he enjoy collecting unpaid bills, but he excelled at it also.

Because of his utterly ruthless nature, it wasn't long before word of his savage exploits had traveled to the ears of the right people.

The people who mattered and looked for qualities like that in a man when considering hiring prospective associates into the certified ranks of the underworld crime families and syndicates.

His reputation preceded him. Once people caught wind of him being on the payroll of any particular loan shark, it wasn't long at all before debt that had been written off, long before, and those guys who had seemed to vanish without a trace, when it came time to pay their bills, started to appear, and settle their accounts, out of thin air, like magic.

That fact, alone, gained him notoriety in the streets. The Boss quickly proved himself to be stand-up and business savvy. Representatives from the leading Irish syndicate had been keeping an eye on the young man who showed them promise and potential. Just like that, it seemed, the doors opened to him, and he walked into the big leagues. The Boss didn't bother with trying to get comfortable. He had plans, big plans.

He wasted no time, when it came to executing his plan, along with anyone else who happened to be in his way. He started killing his way to the top, one adversary at a time. On top of being a stone-cold killer, he was an exceptionally cunning, and brilliant, young man.

He knew his competition and made it a point to quickly ally himself with their enemies. He was a master of manipulation, and it wasn't long before he had the major crime families pegged against one another, in all-out open war.

He had whispered into the ears of the family heads, sowing the seeds of deceit and watching them grow into paranoia, jealousy, and rage.

When one family would fall, due to internal strife, he would appear with his own crew, heavily armed, to "recruit" whoever was left to his cause. He would pick up the pieces, from the aftermath of collapse, and place them into his very own puzzle. He made examples of those who refused his offer. He did not ask twice, and your first answer is your only answer, so choose wisely.

Another thing that set The Boss from the others was his insistence on being present for, if not carrying out himself, the executions of the unfortunates who happened to incite his wrath. Oftentimes, he would choose to oversee the killing not only to ensure the job was handled in a professional manner, but also to make sure the way in which the condemned were disposed of met the gruesome standards of The Boss.

By the year 1979, The Boss controlled the most, if not all, the business in Ireland, Scotland, and Wales. His influence had expanded to reach the United Kingdom and spread throughout most of Europe.

He even had ties in Eastern Canada, he set up shop in Montreal's Old French Quarter, and from there, and he slithered south and worked his way to the West.

He had engineered a fail-proof system, or so it seemed, to encompass all the vices. Prostitution, narcotics, gambling, and loan-sharking, he had his fingers into it all, but there was a balance. Interspersed, throughout it all, was a plethora of legitimate businesses that were meticulously managed and accounted for.

Dirty money was easily laundered and the entire scheme was vastly more successful than The Boss had expected.

The amounts of cash generated and controlled, by all the avenues he had operating, was staggering. Everything he touched seemed to turn to gold; a modern day King Midas. He literally had the luck of the Irish.

By 1983, he had the entire East Coast of the United States on lock. Every major American based, biker gang peddled his wares, helping him expand his reach not only up and down the coast, but Westward too.

Within a relatively short period of time, his influence spanned from the Atlantic Ocean, all the way to the Pacific. He was a regular at the Virgin Islands, and he used them as his getaway, treated them as if the islands were his personal marinas. He demanded respect, and everybody he came in contact with fell in line. His style was old-school mob, all the way. He handed out favors like a bookie hands out tickets. Everyone, from CEO's of multimillion-dollar companies, to politicians, to law-enforcement officials, even to the higher-ups of the government were indebted to him.

The Boss had come from the rough-around-the-edges, twelve year old kid who ran with his Dublin street gang, to the head of his own global empire, responsible for important roles in the importing, exporting, and distribution of tens-of-thousands of tons of narcotics annually.

That, alone, crowned him king, and made him the greatest, non-Hispanic, drug lord in North America. Consequently, that put him in the crosshairs of every cartel from Mexico to Argentina.

Asian organizations, who had their own gambling dens, brothels, and drug trade, didn't think very highly of The Boss and his associates and waged war as they vied for global domination. But, the Asians and the Central American cartels weren't the only organizations who paid attention to what The Boss was doing.

The National Safety Administration and the Department of Defense set a record when posting the reward for the head of The Boss. Eight figures, thanks to the deep pockets of the United States government.

The reward was bigger than that offered for the capture of Osama Ben Laden and James

"Whitey" Bulger, combined. The wanted The Boss badly, and they were willing to pay an ungodly amount to have him taken off the streets, one way or another.

Saint Sinner remembered the day his contact had slid the contract on The Boss across the table and, literally, onto his lap, at the café, like it was yesterday.

It was right after he had amassed his one-hundred-sixty-third professional kill, while on active duty and serving his fourth tour of duty in Fallujah, Iraq. He had been two-weeks into, and eight days away from completion of, his tour.

He had been posted on a rooftop, around the clock, peering through an eight-inch hole and keeping watch over the half-mile kill zone in the shit-hole currently known as Fallujah, when he had received the orders stating he was to be relieved of duty. He hadn't requested, expected, or wanted for that to happen. He had wanted to stay with his brother-in-arms until the end, either until he was killed in action, or until he was on his way home, after the successful completion of his campaign. But, there he sat, across from his contact. "What's this?" he had asked, looking down at his package. The man across from Saint Sinner, whose eyes and most of his face lay hidden behind his aviator glasses, simply replied, "A career change."

The only thing Saint Sinner knew about his contact was that he belonged to one of those "hush-hush" divisions of the N. S. A. The ones that were classified and didn't really exist, spoken about only in whispers and kept in the dark, hidden from most. This man kept tabs on killers, snipers in particular, like a scout for college sports follows players.

He had an offer for Saint Sinner that he really couldn't refuse, an invitation to serve his country doing what he loved; killing bad guys, so he accepted.

The man explained to him that The Boss was the ultimate target, and there was an entire army between him and The Boss. The only way he'd be able to get close enough to the man would be to follow his example and work his way from bottom to top, killing anybody who got in his way.

The contact had related this job to the situation with Pablo Escobar. "Just like that," he said, "take them all out until you have a clear shot. And, by the way, we pay five figures, or better, per job." The nameless, short man in the gray suit could have fit in anywhere. Saint Sinner had no doubt that he'd forget his face the moment he left. They'd end his military career with an honorable death. He was sure there'd be a twenty-one gun salute, at Arlington cemetery, his very own fake grave site and stone, backwards boots on the horse, and all that other fancy stuff you'd see at a military funeral service. But, he wasn't dead yet, and he was trying to keep it that way.

But, that was long ago, and this is now. And, oh how the tables have turned. Now, the hunter had become the hunted. Saint Sinner, angel of darkness, who killed evil men, off the record of course, for the United States National Agenda, was, for the first time, both captured-and-standing face-to-face with The Boss. Two alpha males.

Two apex killers. One bad, the other evil.

Opposite sides of the same coin, and the currency was death. Both men seemed to be sizing one another up, there was nothing sentimental about it, and neither of them appeared to be overly impressed with the other. Now that Saint Sinner really knew the gravity of the situation, and who exactly he was dealing with, he had a little bit of a better idea as to where he was currently located. It turns out his intuition was, yet again, on point. He was somewhere in the Chihuahua Desert. It was rumored, well, maybe it's not so much of a rumor as he thought, that The Boss used this place as his own, private graveyard. In fact, he wasn't the first to decide this particular desert was an ideal location to off bodies.

This spot had been shown to him by a close associate, which is exactly why he liked to use it, and that was as close to sentimental as The Boss would ever get. It was all in the file that the Department of Defense had slipped him, unofficially, historic figures like Al Capone, Billy the Kid, and the James Gang were all said to have been linked to burying people and treasure, too, in and around this very same area back in their day. Train robberies, hold-ups, and wild chases with the United States Calvary were local legends in these parts.

Desolate land, torturous conditions, and isolating from the public and the law, made this place a haven for bad guys who needed to lay-low for a while. Also, in the middle of sniper training, there was always the debate between his fellow peers. Some said that there were ritualistic sacrifices made in the caves of this area. Something about honoring the gods and goddesses, the gate-keepers, of the lay lines, nodes where lines of longitude and latitude are in the right spot, together and opened a door to a parallel universe. A string theory shortcut, or so they said. A pair of mini-black holes next to each other, except they were made from white matter, they said.

Tribesmen and shamans alike had worshipped the same gods, in the same caves, for some two thousand years, or more apart, was proof. Pagans, Native Americans, and even Viking gothics had been to the spot and left their marks. The latter lovingly leaving rough looking slash marks, some people call them runes, one of the first alphabets to have even been used.

Sniper school had been rigorous, ruthless, but it had taught him a lot. His instructor had told him that talking was a way to keep the mind balanced, when you begin to feel the effects of severe dehydration. Desert acclimation training and his anti-terrorism training programs, both, required the soon-to-be snipers to go without water, to experience the delusions and hallucinations that accompany dehydration, so that if they were ever put in a situation like that, they would be able to recognize the sensations and deal with the problem accordingly. Proper preparation prevents piss-poor performance.

They were encouraged to keep a steady flowing stream of discourse to keep their minds busy, distracted from their thirst. Saint Sinner wasn't too sure about how well it worked, but he learned more than he thought he'd ever need to know. Then again, that was twenty years ago. A long time to forget things, to grow soft. But, fortunately for Saint Sinner, he kept up with his conditioning training.

His body was strong, solid, and he was as fierce as he had been, twenty years back.

The Boss and his two goons positioned themselves, along with Saint Sinner, in a crude semblance of a horse shoe around the back of the white van, its rear doors opened. Saint Sinner was still bound at the wrists, unable to stop whatever was about to happen.

He thought about partially charging them with a football style rush, maybe catch them off guard with that, and maybe karate kick one and roundhouse another, but he quickly discard the idea. He knew that would lead to a wild-fire of bullets, he'd end up with a bullet in his foot, or ass, maybe even one in the dick, instead of a clean shot to the head. On second thought, the idea wasn't very appealing, a shot in the crotch?

No thanks.

"So this is how it ends, a round between the eyes and call it a day?" he wondered.

He hung back, waiting, watching for them to make a move, to play their hand. He didn't plan on laying down and dying without a fight, but he didn't want to act too soon and lose any advantage he might have had by being patient. Besides, they had to have something in mind. If they were just going to shoot him dead, they could've done it and planted his body in the Charles River. Something had to give.

Vino nodded, it was like he was trying to suppress a grin. What the fuck was so funny, though? He passed Saint Sinner's elbow to Vasquez, whose catcher's mitt-sized paw clamped onto his forearm, without a word. He seemed to be recalculating Saint Sinner's every breath, his eyes cold, and his face expressionless. He looked like an evil Clint Eastwood, walking and carrying a big stick. He clearly, was the muscle of the group and was fairly intelligent, definitely the one to keep an eye on at all times. Fortunately, the last of the after-effects of whatever drug they had slipped him, were fading away.

Saint Sinner was able to think clearly again, and that feeling of swimming through mud had all but vanished, it had been tapering off while clarity and focus had been restored. But, the boss was also aware of the current situation, he stared at Saint Sinner and said, "Vino, why don't you fetch the gift for our guest?"

Vino grinned ear-to-ear, just like a kid at Christmas, "Sure thing, Boss." He reached into the van and picked up a big box. He set it back down, opened it, and pulled out a second, smaller, box. He spun around, box in hand, and held it up for Saint Sinner's inspection. It looked like it was big enough to hold a basketball, or something around that size, and had no writing on it anywhere.

Saint Sinner began to wonder what might be in the box, but that was when he realized there was thick, red liquid that dripped from the bottom, along the seams. The box was dark, and it was soaked.

Now, everybody was smiling except for Saint Sinner, who already figured out what was in the box. It wasn't rocket science. Again, he eyed the dark, thick-looking liquid as it dripped fat droplets, like tears of a giant child that fell to the ground only to sizzle, and roll a short distance before stopping to collect in the quickly growing puddle below.

His first thought should've been "what's in the box?" but Saint Sinner was no stranger to death and gruesome endings, so immediately he asked himself, "Who – is in the box?"

The Boss was a Kevin Spacey fan, obviously. Saint Sinner had seen that movie with Morgan Freeman and Brad Pitt, the one where Kevin Spacey has a delivery service deliver a box, dripping with blood, to both of the detectives. Morgan Freeman knew what was in that box. The audience, working the movie knew what was in there. Saint Sinner knew, too, but...Fuck! Who did he love, that they had gotten to?

Al, The Boss, stepped around, his back toward the setting sun. His face was shadowed, black as night. His white tracksuit, shades, made him look like the world's most dangerous retiree.

Vino, the human ferret, wearing his black fedora inched to one side, placed the box at Saint Sinner's feet, and then stood by The Boss, clearly satisfied with himself. He was nodding, as if he was playing catch-up on an inside joke, looking at the box, then to Saint Sinner, at Vasquez, and back at the box again, and then to The Boss, over and over.

For a moment, nobody spoke. A moment of silence. The box had the floor at the moment, it seemed. "Well lad, aren't you dying to know what's in that box?" The Boss said, a broad smile forming across his face. Saint Sinner shook his head. No, he wasn't.

The Boss darted a glance at his lackeys and then back at Saint Sinner. For not saying anything, The Boss was clearly understood. Then The Boss spoke, "Maybe I'm Spacey, and you're Brad Pitt, now come and ask me what's in the box, lad, just one time for old Uncle Al, make an old-timer happy. Ask me what is in the box…?"

Saint Sinner frowned, clearly not amused, and said, "I'm not playing along." He thought to himself, "That's exactly what he wants me to do. I won't do it!" But his mind raced ahead of his thoughts, he had one question on his mind: the obvious…

"Who is in that box?"

No sooner had he thought that, and Vasquez decided to help him play along. Vasquez pistol whipped Saint Sinner in the back of his neck, that sweet spot where your spine meets the base of the skull. The blow sent a shock wave through his reflexes, dropping him to his knees. Face-to-face with the wet cornbread square that looked like it came from a bakery. Plain, gray, a new smell tickled his nose, just as Vino said, "When Boss says play along, and you play along!" He was practically leaning over Saint Sinner, now.

The Boss stepped a little bit closer, and in what could have passed as a fatherly tone of voice, he said, "Maybe it comforts you to know, that at this exact moment, six o'clock, on the button," he looked down at his simple, yet classy timepiece, then back, before continuing, "a man, by the name of Jeremiah Brandies, is recovering a box identical to this one, right down to the contents inside.

Saint Sinner was running out of patience, itching to get his hands around any one of their necks. "Patience," his inner guru advised, "just keep them talking while we find a way out of this. He got his feet under him, and he pushed himself up, to a standing position, his wrists still bound.

He said, "Why would I care about some asshole who opens a box with the severed head of his wife inside? And, in case you didn't now, I have no wife, no girl, and no family. So, whoever's head is in this box ate a bullet for nothing."

The Boss snapped, "Head?" A satisfied look found its way to his face, as both his henchmen laughed right along with him, like two puppets with pulled strings. Vasquez gave a silent head-nod, but behind those eyes, Saint Sinner saw murder.

"Okay, what the hell is going on here?" Saint Sinner thought, as he looked again, down at the mystery box, then over at The Boss, who happily began to explain.

"I'm no angel, but give me a little credit, as I'm not a monster either!" The Boss said.
Saint Sinner shook his head and thought to himself, "Yes, yes you are! That's exactly what you are!"

The Boss smiled big and said, "Seven, now there's a movie. Hollywood got it right. Good actors, good plot, great ending, and the climax? Fucking spectacular! Especially if you watch it all the way through, uninterrupted. Isn't that right Vino?"

Vino nodded vehemently, as he said, "Oh yeah, it's top shelf!"

The Boss clapped Vino on the back and smiled. Then he said, "You know why I love that movie, lad?"

Saint Sinner's eyes almost bulged, when he realized that he might know whose head was in that box, "Oh shit!" he thought, the emerald eyed bartender from the Erie Pub! That has to be it! A wave of deep-seated regret washed over him. Melancholy, in such a way it made him think back and regret every word he had said, and every smile he had aimed in her direction.

They must have noticed the friendly banter between the two of them, and now this poor girl's body, and the head it was attached to, before he walked into her work, were separated.

Flirting with the wrong man...He was a selfish screw-up, everyone he met ended up dying? Either by his own hand, or from circumstances related to his association.

He lowered his head, berating himself. Vino crouched down and flipped the top of the box open, and said, "What the... Was he hallucinating?" It's the blood, he thought, it had some kind of a power. He took a deep breath and began to exhale as he looked down, into the box.

"Happy birthday, lad!" The Boss announced, clapping. Vino immediately followed suit, clapping and looking like some sort of a seal soldier in an aquatic army. Vasquez just stood back, watching the procession of events with his steely-eyed scrutiny that made him the scary creep he was.

Saint Sinner anticipated seeing the pair of lifeless green eyes staring back at him, the mouth frozen, and wide open, in a gaping display of horrified shock. The shock brought on by a power saw doing its job, and working it's very through your neck, severing the head from the body. He expected to look and see, the familiar face of the prettiest barkeep in all of Dorchester. He could already hear her voice inside his head, screaming at him thinks like, "This is all your fault! And "Thanks a lot, asshole!" and "How were your free drinks?"

"What the fuck?" Saint Sinner couldn't stop himself from saying, as he looked down, into the box, and saw a birthday cake. Possibly the world's ugliest birthday cake, at that. It was frosted red on red, and had red icing-letters, written in what appeared to have once been cursive writing. The scorching heat had melted the icing, so what the writing said was still a mystery to him.

The cake, as a whole, was beginning to look more like a soup than a cake. It was a mess. The only remaining letter was still legible, was big "H" and everything else was just a big mess.

The whole thing was a bloody-red mess, but it definitely was not a head in that box. He was relieved as much as he was confused. He couldn't help but wonder why he ended up getting a shiner like that, if no blood had been spilled? It made no sense to him.

The feeling he had had in the pit of his stomach led him to believe that surely someone had been hurt, badly. Anybody who has spilled blood before is familiar with that feeling in the air, around them. It was intoxicating. Heavy, and dangerous.

This was the worst birthday surprise he had ever received in his entire forty years alive, and he had had some pretty terrible ones, in the past. But, this "Seven" themed box, in the middle of the desert, topped them all.

Saint Sinner narrowed his eyes, as Vino began to laugh a rough, grating laugh. Vasquez went as far as to plaster a fake smile on his face, a smile that didn't touch his eyes.

He hated Vasquez, everything about him. Especially his arrogant, cocky, mannerisms. He thought "if this prick doesn't take me out while my hands are tied, I'm going to enjoy killing that one. " But, Saint Sinner was beginning to feel like Vasquez had something other than the mercy of a well-placed bullet, in store for him, something dark. There would be no such thing as a quick or painless death, if Vasquez had his way.

"What, lad, did you expect something different?" The Boss said, with a smile, "Did you think

I was a heartless monster?" The Boss shifted his weight to his other leg, still smiling, he continued, "I bet you thought I'd gone and snatched up the pretty, little mouse, who served you your birthday drinks the other night, did you not?"

The Boss shook his head and said, "You know, O'Connor's daughter Emily?" Saint Sinner set his jaw and gritted his teeth, but didn't say a word. "Oh I did give it some thought, don't get me wrong, but then I realized it would be such a waste of such a valuable asset," The Boss said.

Saint Sinner arched an eyebrow at that, a look of interest and slight confusion plain on his face. The Boss seemed to get a rise out of the look on his face, nodding, he carried on, "She's a perfectly good wench, who I can count on to get this job done, and done right. For example, if I ever decided that I needed to have something slipped into a drink, or if I need anything at all, for that matter, she'll be there to cater to my every whimsical fancy.

Saint Sinner shook his head, clearly disappointed with what he was hearing. The Boss's smile grew a little wider at that, and he said, "I realize, lad, that you only care for yourself, and that you're a big, bad, tough-guy contract killer and all that other nonsensical garbage that you attribute to yourself, and because of that, it would be doubly wasteful for me to have taken her out.

Utterly disappointed, Saint Sinner started connecting the dots in his mind, "So it was the booze, after all, I knew it. But Emily, really? I still don't know if I believe it. But, I guess, that would make a lot more sense than the Snapple being tampered with, that would take an unrealistic stroke of luck to accomplish."

Also, the Greeks who owned that liquor store, weren't affiliated with The Boss. As far as Saint Sinner knew, they ran in separate crowds.

The odds of the two Greek brothers taking orders from an Irishman, or anyone for that matter, were slim to none. But, then again, you can never really be sure about something like that. Especially in the underworld.

"Just stay cool, "Saint Sinner told himself. "Vasquez is just looking for a reason, any reason, to shove that pointed boot of his up your ass, and on top of that, the sun's going down."

"You're already up shit creek, without a paddle, don't jump out of the boat and make it worse. Save yourself the trouble, and play along," Vino said, seemingly trying to sound like a concerned friend, more so than one of his captors.

"Spare me your bleeding heart routine," Saint Sinner said, looking The Boss in the eyes, "according to the New York Times, you're responsible for the bombing of a building in Costa Rica. All that, to simply eliminate a rival of yours who happens to smuggle cocaine.

One, who just so happened to be running the major smuggling routes, underground highways and tunnels, that run all the way through Central America and into the United States, right past the southern bordering states, where Trump is building his wall at the moment."

Right then, Vino interrupted Saint Sinner, "So what? What's your point?"

Saint Sinner looked from The Boss, over at Vino, and back again before adding, "Twenty-three innocent people, civilians, died in that apartment complex, that day. And, *somebody*" he made it a point to emphasize the word, while maintaining eye contact with The Boss, letting him know, for sure, that he knew exactly what went down, "had to have paid off the authorities, because when the official incident report was released, the bombing was referred to as an unfortunate explosion.

"Eleven of the twenty three people that died that day were children." A moment passed before anybody spoke. The Boss broke the silence, a dark grin, from ear to ear, sinister in every sense of the word, "I guess I made those cartel fellows think twice about messing with an old man, like myself, now didn't I?"

His tone was matter of fact, and his voice was low. This time, it was The Boss's eyes that were narrowed. "Violence, in their mother's neighborhood, is a message they understand. Respect, even. War, sometimes, equals peace lad, you know that. Who exactly, do you think you're fooling now, anyway" You, single handedly, have killed more people than the entire National Guard has in the past ten years. I'm talking about the whole branch of the service lad. So, spare – me - the – tears for the children act. Now how about a slice of cake, for the birthday boy?'

"My pleasure, Boss, one slice of cake, coming right up!" Vino replied, starting to cut the cake.

"Saint Sinner shook his head hard, and said, "No, thank you. You know what you can do with that cake, don't you?"

Vino stopped what he was about to do, looking from Saint Sinner, to The Boss, unsure whether to continue. "Do I have to spell it out for you?" Saint Sinner said, a hint of a smile forming.

The Boss frowned, and started to walk around the side of Saint Sinner, toward Vasquez, who was currently making sure Saint Sinner was under control, thanks to the gun that was wedged firmly between his shoulders.

The Boss then said, "You have a bad attitude, lad. Alas, yes, I know exactly what I can do with it. I can share it with your loved ones. Oh wait, you don't have any family. Your whore of a mother decided that she'd rather play with her Barbie dolls than with you. She dropped you off, like a bag of trash, didn't she? Which, in the end, is exactly where she ended up, herself, dead."

The two men locked eyes, both smiling. One's smile was genuine, the other was forced. Saint Sinner's blood began to boil. If he was the incredible hulk, he would have, just then, turned into the mean, green, fighting, machine and crushed the old man like the cockroach he truly was.

Saint Sinner couldn't think of anyone else he hated more than he hated the miserable prick standing in front of him, right then. It hurt to hear, because it was all true. Apparently, he wasn't the only one who did their homework. The Boss, like himself had a collection about people's lives, like kids collect baseball cards. But, it was true, Saint Sinner's mother was dead to him, just like that awful cake was.

The Boss, Vasquez, and Saint Sinner, all watched Vino, as he whistled while he picked up where he left off. He carved a crude looking piece from the cake, dropped it onto a disposable, plastic paint tray, and waved it in front of Saint Sinner's face. It was about an inch, or so, away from his mouth and nose, so close, he could smell the sugary-sweet frosting.

The up-close and personal presence of food reminded him of how hungry he was, but no matter how hungry he was, he was resolved to not eat that cake.

As usual, everybody, with the exclusion of Vasquez, had a shit-eating grin on their faces. Especially Vino, who began taunting Saint Sinner with that damned slice of cake. He waved it all around, making airplane sounds, and brought it right back to under his nose, meanwhile, saying things like, "open wide," and, "coming in for a landing." Saint Sinner was not amused, or impressed, by Vino's antics.

Saint Sinner spit at Vino, once he got close again, hitting him square in the face and dripping from his nose. The world froze. Vino was momentarily stunned, he just stood there, his mouth ajar, as if about to say something.

The Boss looked on, tilting his head, watching the saliva gather at the tip of Vino's nose, waiting for it to slide down, and fall to the ground. Just then Vino recovered from his momentary stupor, he whipped out his forty-five caliber, and shoved it in Saint Sinner's face.

"Motherfucker spit on me!" Vino yelled, "Cock sucking, two balled, bitch-ass, motherfucker!

Can I shoot this asshole Boss?

Let me shoot this son-of-a-whore!

Please?

In the most fatherly way he could have, like a scout master teaching a merit badge lesson to his group of boy scouts, The Boss said, "No son, we'd better not stoop to his level," he looked over at the seething Saint Sinner, and then at Vino.

They looked like two junkyard dogs, nose-to-nose, about to tear each other to shreds. "And to think he goes by 'Saint' Sinner. That wasn't very saintly, now was it lad?" The Boss said, "This man has a chip on his shoulder, and bad manner to boot! Obviously he didn't have a proper upbringing with loving parents to teach him wrong from right.

So, no Vino, this one only had a junkie, who turned tricks for old Rocky Sanders, a.k.a. 'the Sword-man' or 'Sandman.' I don't know how he got the first, but the second he earned, for having the perfect heroin he sold. That's what people would say, anyway. I wouldn't know, I never used drugs myself, and usually just off junkies, when I know I can get away with it. They're a waste of life, in the truest sense."

Vasquez nodded, seemingly in agreement with The Boss. "Nope, lads, this fella, here, wasn't worth mommy's time, so, I guess it's up to us to play 'daddy' for a while, and teach him that it's wrong to spit in the face of his host, especially when all they were doing, was trying to show him some god-damned hospitality.

Apparently, your own daddy didn't care enough to show you…oh, that's right! You don't even know who your father is! Because your mommy was a junkie-whore! I have a guess at who it might be, though." He stepped a little bit closer to Saint Sinner, "Old Sandman" was a big fella, much like yourself. I saw a photo of him once, wasn't easy to get, mind you, I had to pay off a retired homicide detective, call in a favor. You know, most of the people from our time are dead, dying, or going crazy. You and old 'Sandman' have the same eyes, lad," The Boss grinned. "So tell me, how does it feel to know that your daddy was whoring out your mommy, all full of dope?"

In the blink of an eye, Saint Sinner dove towards The Boss, head first, a guttural roar coming from somewhere deep inside of him, primal rage had taken control of him. But, his charge was cut short. Vasquez, who was standing right behind him, had been waiting for him to do something like that, and, unfortunately, he reacted immediately. Vasquez hammered Saint Sinner in the back of his head with the butt of his gun, taking him down to his knees. Saint Sinner, panting heavily, through gritted teeth, said, "I'm… going… to… kill… you!"

The Boss appeared to be amused by the futile attempt made on his life, and at the ah-so predictable choice of words that followed that failed attempt. He laughed, saying, "If you could have, you would have, lad. Come on, now, up you go. It'll be dark soon, and we have a hike to take." The Boss started to walk off, following a trail that led somewhere to the South.

Once The Boss had gone a little ways, Vino swiftly kicked Saint Sinner, who was still recovering from the near concussion he had gotten a moment prior, in the gut, "Whoops!" he said, smiling his stupid smile of his. Saint Sinner stumbled in the wrong direction, but not for long, before Vino grabbed his semi-free arm, pistol still jammed into his back. "Hold him a second, Vino said to Vasquez, I need to get that thing out of the van." He walked over the van, and he pulled out a large canvas hockey bag. Something inside the bag was making metallic clanging noises. "Shovels, probably," Saint Sinner thought. Vino carried the bag in both arms, but his feet were free to kick Saint Sinner with, and so he did, right in the lower-back. "March!" he ordered.

That kick was a wakeup call of sorts, and as he moved forward, he swore to himself that he would remember to think about it later, when he was somehow ending Vino's life. But, as for right now, he was still alive, so he reluctantly complied and kept it moving.

Four shadows marched, single file, down the sloping desert trail. They made their own way through many cacti, the ones that look as if they're being held up by robbers, you know, hands in the air, as the infamous Boss led them along, and almost cheerily he had a spring to his step.

Small, matchbox car-sized reptiles zigzagged from rock to rock, dashing underfoot, pausing briefly to roll an eye around before scurrying off, under the cover of shrubbery that had thorn-filled tangles.

The minutes felt like hours as they continued their journey. Progressively, the terrain changed. Small rocks turned into larger rocks, and those turning to boulders. The path itself became treacherous, stories that could easily sprain ankles were strewn about, and sand pits made for slow-going. The whole ordeal upset Vino, he continued to prod Saint Sinner with the barrel of his gun, and complain while he did it. "Move it, asshole!" Vino demanded, kicking Saint Sinner again. Saint Sinner smiled, on the inside, through the pain, because he knew that karma was a bitch, and that Vino definitely had it coming.

Vino seemed to be having a hard time keeping up with the brisk pace that The Boss had set, that was why he kept messing with Saint Sinner. It gave him a chance to catch his breath, and it made him think he was earning his way into The Boss's appreciation by roughing up the captive. "Slow down again, and I'll shoot you in the foot, I'll shoot your toe off, how's that sound?" He asked, huffing and puffing, "You want to lose a toe?"

Keep moving.

"Hey Vasquez," Vino said, "Why did you say we had to worry about this guy? He's not that tough, if you ask me." The Boss stopped for a second and looked like he was about to say something, but decided against it and kept going. Vasquez smirked at Vino, then glanced over at Saint Sinner, chewing the stub of his Camel cigarette.

The look on Vazquez's face told Saint Sinner everything he needed to know. He had just let him know that he knew Vino was the weak link in the chain. It also told Saint Sinner that it was almost that time. Time to say goodbye to this world, and everything in it.

The look on the face of Vasquez was somewhere between "you and me have some unfinished business to attend to" and "I've read your resume' of death, now let's see if you're the real deal." The Boss moved with a nimbleness that belied his age.

The Boss was in excellent physical condition, aside from his slight limp, you'd never believe the man was seventy-two years old.

Saint Sinner had picked up on the limp right away. He always paid attention to detail, but he doubted that either Vino or Vasquez even noticed that their boss favored his left leg. That just goes to show you the difference in the level of professionalism between Saint Sinner and your everyday goons.

The sun was hanging low in the western, afternoon sky. The brilliant reds and oranges, from before, gave way to shades of violet, across the darkening horizon. The desert sand sparkled in the last light of the day, bright colors being reflected here and there. It looked like it had rained diamonds, instead of water, down on the plain, and there they sat, just waiting to be plucked from the Earth by the greedy, grasping, fingers of man.

Saint Sinner took a deep breath, captivated by the beauty of it all, then let it go. He decided it was as good a time as ever to make peace with himself. "It's a good day to die," he thought. It all made sense to him now, why killers, in the past, would go out of their way to make sure the job was done or choose this place to make their last stand. It was so beautiful here. The sky was a canvas of color, and the desert was an ocean of brilliance that glittered under the first stars of the soon-to-be-night and the moon was already hanging low and rising.

Saint Sinner took a mental picture of the magnificent landscape before him, blinking in and out with each step.

It was something his mind has always done automatically, storing the photos for a dark time of need. The ways things were looking, such a time could be right around the corner.

"Almost there, lads," The Boss announced, like an evil tour guide. The boulders were clustered closer together, as they began to descend, down the canyon's gradually sloping wall. Larger, now that they were closer, they could see the openings in the face of the mountain. The entrances to caves, no doubt, varying in size. Some were only the span of a few feet, others were gargantuan.

These caves looked like they could've been dwellings from long, long, ago. From the Bronze Age, maybe. Ruins, waiting to be found and used once again. They seemed very similar to Colorado's Mesa Verde's Anastasi tribes, cave-dwelling people, who made homes out of the natural rock-face cliffs, carving out housing complexes that would protect them from predators and the elements, all in one. Anybody seeking shelter would have jumped at the chance to live in these caves.

The Boss called a stop to the march in front of one of the largest openings, it was easily thirty feet across, "this is it," he said. "Vasquez, keep an eye on our guest, while Vino fetches a spade from the bag." Vino looked confused, "A spade boss?" The Boss shook his head, disappointed, yet again, he said, "Vino, Vino, Vino...," he smiled.

"If your father hadn't shown me devotion and loyalty, like he did, back during prohibition, I would have had you put down a long time ago." Vino's eyes lowered to the ground, "I'm sorry, Boss."

The Boss said, "Yes, you are. However don't apologize, not for your own stupidity. Listen to me, you dim-witted fool, it's obvious that we can't have him dig his own grave with his bare hands.

The stone would be very difficult for him to get through with only his poor hands to do so, though I admit, it would be entertaining to see him try."

The Boss looked towards Saint Sinner for a moment, perhaps he was entertaining the idea, "Alas, we don't have time for all of that." He looked back at Vino, then to Vasquez, "But while we're here, boys, we're going to hook two fish at once. There's something I want to check out inside this cave. There's an old legend about some rubbish the History Channel was talking about, claiming ancient powers and the like. Just an outdated rumor, no doubt, but this is it. I'm not getting any younger. Even, I, know my time at the top of the cash pile, is limited. If the rumor proves true, I'll turn this place into my own, personal Disney Land. More importantly, though, it will put an end to my wondering about the whole situation."

Saint Sinner thought about the chink in Al's armor he had discovered: he was superstitious, then his eyes fell upon the cave's entrance. Vino said, "Well excuse me Boss. Wouldn't treasure hunters, like those old school pioneers, mountain men, or those gold-fevered miners have gotten ahold of any treasure lying around by now?" Nodding, The Boss replied, "Nobody's going to leave a big score sitting around for centuries, but this isn't any normal treasure. It's a doorway of some kind, a portal, they said, a gateway to another time and place.

Stonehenge, the Bermuda Triangle, the pyramids, the fountain of youth, that sort of treasure. A node. Their latitude and longitude holds astrological significance, according to those two atom smashing idiots at C.E.R.N. Lay Lines, this is a place like those. It's hidden inside somewhere. Unfortunately the men who stumbled upon that tip all had accidents with knives, while sleeping in their beds. Crazy coincidence, and messy.

Vasquez?'

"Yeah, boss?" Vazquez turned his attention from Saint Sinner to the Boss, awaiting further instruction.

"Be on point, it's about time we get started," the Boss said, looking at Vino, he added, "Vino, let's get started." Vino dropped the canvas bag, unzipped it, and from inside, he produced two shovels, a pickaxe, and several flashlights. Next, out came the Coleman Lanterns, and a bundle of rope. Once done unpacking, Vino pulled his forty-five from the holster on his hip and pointed its barrel back at Saint Sinner.

"Now lad," the Boss said, stepping in front of Saint Sinner, looking at him directly, "Let me make things crystal clear for you, before we begin our fun adventure. Vino?" Vino perked up.

"Yes, Boss?"

The Boss continued, "Didn't you always dream of becoming a surgeon, back when you were just a wee lad?"

Vino smiled at that, "You bet I did, Boss, I used to pretend I was a doctor all the time. It has been a very long time, though. I could definitely use some practice." He unsheathed his knife and made exaggerated zigzagging cuts through the air, all the while, a youthful gleam in his eyes.

The Boss nodded, looking back at Saint Sinner, he said, "Get my drift?" Saint Sinner nodded, then looked up at the sky one last time before they decided to drag him into the dark confines of the cave. He saw a red tailed hawk riding the currents in the air. It circled three times before it flew off the North.

That had to have been an omen if he ever did see one. He decided to continue biding what little time he had left, quietly. He figured if he remained quiet and withdrawn, they would believe him to be defeated, and resigned to his fate.

"Now," the Boss said, "do you want to work, or die?" as he smiled his signature white, toothy, smile. "Make no mistake though, either way you choose to go, you'll be dying, but one option will allow you to keep sucking air for little while longer."

It almost sounded like they were discussing a casual business agreement, and in a way they were. How did Saint Sinner want to spend his last moments on Earth? Digging his own grave out of the unyielding sandstone under his feet, or lying dead, his body cooling while the pit was dug out for him?

He was tempted to tell them all to fuck themselves, to let them slave in the heat to hide his mutilated corpse, but he knew that would only hasten the process of his demise. He could beat them, but to do so, he would have to remain cool, calm, and collected.

"What's it going to be lad? Daylight's a burning', the Boss said.

Saint Sinner knew that The Boss was a sadistic bastard at heart, and was the type of guy that read books on the Spanish Inquisition's torture methods, back in medieval times, just too simply broaden his wicked horizons. He needed more time. He needed to get free. That meant he needed to play ball. "I'll work, just make my ending a quick one, once the time comes, that's all I ask," Saint Sinner said. "I'm tired of this world, anyway."

The Boss squinted his eyes, staring at Saint Sinner, as he calculated a dozen different plans for what would come next. Saint Sinner had no doubt that The Boss knew of his extensive military training. He, no doubt, knew that Saint Sinner was almost as deadly unarmed as he was with a gun in hand. He – did - know, and The Boss would be watching him closely. Especially with this sudden change of attitude. Saint Sinner wouldn't be getting over on him again, The Boss thought, as he watched the bound man attempt to appear as though he had no will left to live. This man had become a serious fucking problem in the past few months. Thirty four of The Boss's underlings had met their end at the hands of Saint Sinner.

Men, who had made The Boss rich, running his rackets all across the globe. Finally, The Boss had found it impossible to carry on business as usual. He had to handle the problem, and here he was sitting in front of him, ready to die.

"That's a good, lad, "The Boss said, holding the gaze of Saint Sinner, his grin returning. "I knew you'd say that. But, know this, your little plan won't be working. You can buy yourself a little time, but you can't afford to buy back your life."

Both Vino and Vasquez stiffened at hearing The Boss's last remark, as if the thought had never crossed their minds. "It's okay though," The Boss continued, "by yourself the time. Lie to yourself, convince yourself that you're good enough to pull off a daring escape, one last time. Please, there's nothing I love more than watching the death of hope in a man's eyes when he finally realizes that the end has come. It's like a recreational drug to me, lad, it gets me high."

The Boss walked around, to the other side of Saint Sinner, "I know all about you, lad. Army ranger, and not just the point-and-shoot type, either. An intelligence officer, smart, and useful, enough to be recruited by the N. S. A., to run a division of the organization, once your contract was up. You turned it down though, didn't you? Wanted to continue doing what you really enjoy, killing. You certainly have a knack for it, and a style I can't help but admire. A real workaholic, but, unfortunately, you work for the wrong side.

That must be how you rationalize living the type of life, lad, by thinking you're working for the 'good guys.' Well, let me tell you, sonny, they're more corrupt than I ever was! The blood money they collect, from oil alone, makes my operation look like a lemonade stand.

You and I, we're not so different.

You're a killer for hire. For the past eighteen months, you've been taking out my upper-staff, hoping to get a shot at my handsome face. Ah, lad, you've been like a wolf in the hen house.

That last one you killed really got my attention," The Boss laughed, crazily would be an understatement, "sending a bullet through the only gap in a solid steel door?

Genius!

You planted that mother fucker right in Big Timba's brain. Somehow, you discovered his habit of verifying the faces of his visitors, himself, through the peep-hole. Even, I, overlooked that! Bravo!"

The Boos shook his head, "if the situation was different, "he looked almost regretful. "I'd pay you whatever you asked to have you work for me, but after all this ruckus, I could never let you get away with it.

 Not to mention, I'd never be able to trust you. And, the hundred million dollars, on my head, is just too much of an incentive. Not that anyone is capable of pulling off such a feat. I've already made sure that anyone that could even come close to succeeding has been taken care of. Some people are too stupid, or too impulsive for their own good."

The Boss took a moment to read Saint Sinner's face. The lack of surprise, at the mention of the bounty, confirmed The Boss's suspicions. Only a few in the world, could offer such a high bounty. The list was incredibly short, the N. S. A., M16, or potentially some D. O. D., rehash cover, but it amounted to the same thing.

Far above, in the sky, another red tailed hawk called out. Saint Sinner looked up just in time to catch it circle around once and move on. A slight breeze could be felt, coming from the cave's entrance. That told Saint Sinner that there had to be another entrance to the cave in front of him, somewhere.

"Vino?" The Boss changed tact.

"Yes, Boss?" Vino replied, kicking at a lizard, but the little lizard was too fast for him.

"Cut the ties on our friend's wrists, and do be careful. Also, hand him a shovel," The Boss ordered.

Vino was face to face with Saint Sinner, but only for a moment, but it was long enough for him to whisper, "I'm going to use my scalpel, first, to operate on your eyes. That'll make things more interesting, huh? You'll never know what I'm going to operate next!"

Saint Sinner nodded slightly, and took a mental note to definitely kill Vino first, and to use his own knife to do it.

The ties were cut.

Saint Sinner rubbed his wrists, where the ties had been letting the blood flow back into his hands, as he watched the laser pointer circling on the zipper of his jeans. "Don't worry, I'm N. R. A. certified," Vasquez said, nonchalantly, as he set his sights on Saint Sinner's family jewels. "I'm great with moving targets, too, thanks to my dad. He taught me a coin trick when I was a kid.

He would flip a silver dollar up high, over his head, and with a .22 rifle, I was expected to hit the coin, dead-center. "In God We Trust" was supposed to take a perfect semi-circle around the entry hole. I practiced for years, from age seven to fourteen, before I hit my first bulls-eye. There's a certain knack to hitting a moving target, I'm sure you know that, though.

I saw all those marksmanship medals you had on your dress uniforms in your downstairs closet."

Saint Sinner maintained a flat affect, not letting Vasquez know that he was surprised to find out about the scumbag being inside his townhouse, poking through his wardrobe.

In his wardrobe hung seven custom-tailored Brooks Brother's suits, all ironed and organized by day of the week he would wear them. There was also his formal, green dress uniform, for parades that he hadn't worn since his last trip to the White House, to consult with a friend, who called in a favor, on a security matter. The same friend that lined him up with his last mission.

He filed that thought somewhere in the back of his mind, as he thought about that day after

9/11, when in-house killers were all suspect until they could figure out who the mastermind behind the attack, was. They pinned it on camel-riding, towel headed bad guys who shit in the desert and wipe with their bare hands. Ones who slept in caves and bounced around from village to village.

Foreign.

Different.

They were strangers in a strange land, invading holy lands like the Knights Templar, thousands of years ago. And, these sand dwelling tribesmen were still there, warriors in their own rite.

They were just scary enough to convince the American people that few Middle-Eastern rebels, now called terrorists, were responsible for the greatest attack on America since Pearl Harbor. It was the videos on the internet, of United States citizens being beheaded, that really sold it, though.

The general public fell for the story hook, line, and sinker. They ate it up, and worked themselves into a righteous fury, ushering in a new age of security, which gave the national agency carte blanch, and a never-ending budget to play with.

Overnight it seemed, the N. S. A., and the C. S. S., the Central Security Service, were abounding in wealth and opened doors.

The videos, promoting the "Death to America" theme, went viral, and stirred up every John and Jane in the United States. They took the attack personally, hatred welling up inside them, as they shouted dumbly at the aggressor, the target that had so conveniently been pointed out to them.

Meanwhile, the real evil geniuses behind 9/11 were just getting warmed up. That was exactly why he had set the trap. Saint Sinner highly doubted that The Boss had friends in his network, especially friends that deep in the mix, but, the M1-6 contact was close enough.

And, now, this cowboy with a death wish just received the distinguished honor of being made-man number two. Saint Sinner would be showing this man no mercy when the time came to delete him from the face of the earth, right after Vino was taken care of, of course. He might even use the same knife on both clowns.

"Here you go," Vino said, handing Saint Sinner the shovel, "where do you want the grave at, Boss?"

The Boss looked at Vino, rolled his eyes, and said, "Grave...," he chuckled, "don't be so dramatic. Right where he's standing is a mighty fine place, just as good as any other, I suppose. Vasquez, just keep that thing pointed right where it is," he gestured to the gun in Vasquez's hand, then nodded toward Saint Sinner, "and, if he so much as blinks in an aggressive manner, well, pretend you're duck hunting and he's the first mallard of the season."

The Boss grinned, and Vasquez nodded, "Yes, sir." Turning his attention back to Saint Sinner, The Boss continued, "Now, would be a good time to start digging, lad, if you stop, even for just one second, I'm going to start counting.

For each second of rest that I see you take, I'll be increasing my number by one. If, it so happens, I reach the number ten...Believe me, you'd rather not know that I will be granting Vino's wish, and allowing him to practice being the surgeon he always wanted to be."

The Boss winked at Vino, and Vino smiled a sinister smile and said, "You know, I could probably manage to string out your death for at least a day or two, maybe even three because you're a strong one.

A man can endure a lot more pain when he's a tough guy. The human body is far more resilient than most people believe, do you have any idea how long it'll take before your organs start to fail?" vino looked over at Saint Sinner, apparently waiting for an answer to the rhetorical question. After about thirty seconds, he continued, "Me neither. We'll know soon enough, though."

Saint Sinner said nothing. He just listened to all the nonsense, in one ear and out the other. He decided to get to work, stabbing at the hard, crusty-top of the desert floor. He swung the shovel around and discarded the heap of sand and rocks somewhere to the side. He was digging his own grave, and he knew it, but it had to be done.

In the meantime, in between time, he would be plotting and planning, scheming a way to turn the grave he was digging into his captor's grave, instead of his own.

The Boss's henchmen took up positions on either side of him as he slowly chipped away at the appointed task at hand. Their eyes were focused, and their trigger-fingers were ready. Ready to kill.

The Boss stepped closer to Vasquez, leaned in, and whispered something in his ear. Saint Sinner couldn't hear what was said, but The Boss looked appeased, and he started to whistle. It sounded like it might have been an Irish folk song, as he casually walked away, toward the cave's massive entrance.

The Boss set foot into the cave, his head looking left, right, and all around, trying to use the last of the failing sunlight to his benefit, trying to take in the scene around him.

The sand was still hot as hell from baking in the cruel sun all day long. The heat emanated from it, causing Saint Sinner to drip sweat profusely from the exertion of digging that damned hole nonstop. It dripped into his eyes, stinging, and into his mouth.

As time elapsed the strange sphere in the sky had finally found its resting place, below the horizon. Fortunately, for Saint Sinner, with the sun down, the temperature started to drop slightly. It wasn't much, but he was grateful for it. Stars began to twinkle and shine, in the twilight sky, and the nearly full moon was breathtaking. With the moon as big, and as bright as it was, it was still easy to see everything around him. It wasn't dark enough yet to warrant a flashlight.

The Boss had been gone for a short while now, and was presumably far enough out of earshot. Saint Sinner knew the time to act was upon him.

He needed to pick a fight with the two minions before he dug too deep and ended up stuck in the hole he was digging.

He needed to take their minds off of him long enough to make one good shot, one that counted. He would make sure it did, too. His life depended on it. In his mind, he was trying to determine which of the two were the weakest. At first, he had thought Vino, but now, he wasn't so sure. They both had their own strengths and weaknesses. Saint Sinner was running out of time and needed to make up his mind. Who was it going to be, Vino or Vasquez?

"Which of these two clowns would be easier for me to get worked up into a shit-fit" Saint Sinner thought, looking back, over his shoulders, as he shoveled his way closer and closer to his own demise.

He decided that there was really only one way to find out, "Vino…," he said, "don't let The Boss go too far all by himself. The legends are about evil spirits who inhabit these caves. They're true, by the way, and he's more than likely in danger right now. But then again, I'm sure a cultured man, like yourself, already knew all that.

Vino glanced toward the cave entrance The Boss had entered, a nervous look on his homely face. The Boss was clearly not in sight, he was somewhere in that cave, searching for God knows what.

Saint Sinner started counting, in his head, as soon as Vino turned to look for The Boss. Once Vino had brought his attention back to Saint Sinner, four seconds had elapsed in total. So, Saint Sinner figured that left a solid two-second, window for him to have done whatever he had wanted. He could do a lot with only two seconds. But, was he sure of himself, or simply overconfident? The Boss allowing him to be untied-and-giving him a shovel, which could easily be used as a weapon, increased his odds of survival by about eleven percent, or so, he figured. That, added to what he had already estimated his odds to eat, put him somewhere around the fourteen percent mark.

He'd have to move very fast.

"Hey Vasquez, what's a smart man like you, doing, pulling low henchmen duty for a senior citizen, like The Boss? He's looking to retire. There's no future with him," Saint Sinner said, watching him out of the corners of his eye, and waiting for some kind of reaction or response. But, Vasquez didn't take the bait. He didn't even blink. "Well that settles that," Saint Sinner thought, "Vino, it is."

He looked over at Vino, wiping the sweat from his brow, and said, "Vino, do you realize that Vasquez is going to have to kill you sooner or later, right? When The Boss retires, like he's already been talking about, you'll be done, too. Last time I checked, there was no retirement plan for low-level coffee fetcher, like you, once he sells the farm and moves into the bad-guy retirement home, of his choice.

Vasquez, here, will be his guy, and his first order will be to silence any weak links that could potentially connect him to his old criminal enterprises. Anyone who knows the intimate details, on any of the dirt, has to go. You know, things like where The Boss lives, stash houses, contact names, or really any information that could be sold and used against him if, let's say, somebody offered you a billion dollars to turn on your boss."

Vino just smiled at Saint Sinner, shaking his head. "Nice try, nobody would ever pay a billion bucks for The Boss. Not even for the president. Not for anyone!"

Saint Sinner scoffed, "Oh yeah? Then what do you think about the one hundred million dollar bounty that's currently being offered to anyone willing and able to put an eighty-six cent slug into the old man's skull? It's open to all takers, even you! All you'd need to do is dump a couple into him, and then head to the bank to cash the biggest fucking check you've ever seen."

Vino snapped, "Bullshit!"

Saint Sinner shook his head and continued, "That's enough for you and me to split evenly. Fifty million dollars each. We can split it. I'm a man of my word, Vino. I'll take you to get your money, myself.

Hell, the people I work for will pay you for offing the top target on their list. You'll see millions more in contracts, before the day is even over. You could work fulltime for them.

Think about security! What I'm offering you Vino...Fifty million dollars in cold, hard, cash. All you have to do is shoot the Marlboro man, here, in the head. We'll go and get The Boss together!

That is, unless you want to keep being his bitch, and getting paid next to nothing, until he has you dig your own grave because you know too much for the old man to play shuffle board with a clear conscience.

You're just a worm to him. He's going to toss you out when he's done with you, Vino. I can tell. He won't do it personally, of course. He'll have Vasquez, here, cut your throat, or blast you in the back. Look at his face, Vino. It's all true! It's true, isn't it Vasquez?"

An uncomfortable silence filled the air, as Vino looked back and forth, between Saint Sinner and Vasquez. For a moment, the wind picked up, and with it, came a light dusting of sand that covered everything in their vicinity with a coat of light-colored, fine desert sand.

Vasquez kicked one of his boots against the other, in order to clear the sand that had amassed, meanwhile, staring through narrowed eyes at Saint Sinner.

Time was running out. The hole he was digging was already almost as deep as he was tall. Saint Sinner scooped another small pile of dirt and rocks into his shovel, making the pit deeper, still, he tossed it aside, and slyly said, "I give you another ninety days, tops, Vino.

Once I'm dead, it's over for you.

You heard The Boss, he said it himself, and he knows his time at the top of the game is over. Guys like him are very thorough, believe me, Vino. I've been taking them out professionally for years now. Bad guys, like him, are all the same. They don't take chances. They kill people that know too much. Especially errand boys, like yourself, that don't bring in the big bucks for The Boss. You don't add zeros to his bank accounts, unless, of course you take into consideration the money you cost him, but those are zeroes in the wrong places.

Now, point that pistol at Vasquez, the-real-threat, and pull the trigger! I'm trying to save your life, man! Fifty million dollars, Vino! Kill him, Vino! Kill him, Vino!" Saint Sinner emptied another shovel-scoop, as he watched Vino process the information, he could almost literally see the wheels turning in Vino's head, fear and panic kicking in, confusion plain on his face.

Vasquez had had enough. "Shut the fuck up!" Vasquez spat.

That was the cue Saint Sinner was waiting for, "You see, Vino, he doesn't want you to know! Ask him! Look into his eyes, look at his face! Ask him if The Boss ever told him to be ready, whenever necessary, to snuff you out and throw your ass into an unmarked, shallow grave, probably somewhere right around here. Shit, this hole I'm digging could easily fit two bodies into it, now that I think about it. I have a gut feeling, Vino, and my gut never leads me astray."

Vasquez's blood began to boil, "I said, SHUT THE FUCK UP!" he yelled.

"Ask him Vino!"

"Just ask him!" Saint Sinner prodded.

Vasquez narrowed his eyes even more, set his jaw, his mouth was a thin line. He refocused his sights on Saint Sinner's crotch, trigger finger itching.

Vino's gun wavered, slowly sinking, lower and lower. He looked over at Vasquez, a strange combination of dismay and courage on his face, but most of all, he looked hurt.

Vino turned, fully facing Vasquez, now. He took a deep breath, to steady himself, before pointing his forty-five at Vasquez, all of a sudden sure of himself, "Is it true? I need to know, Vasquez, don't fuck with me!" Vino's voice was all accusation, "Huh! Did you and The Boss have a conversation about clipping me, once he retires? Is that what you two were doing down in Fort Lauderdale, is that why he bought the warehouse there? Huh? Answer me!"

Vasquez shook his head in a disgusted manner, "Why you dirty son-of-a-bitch!" He was glaring at Saint Sinner, if looks could kill, they would have.

"Answer me, god damn it, is it true?!" Vino shouted, his hands shaking.

"Yes, Vino, it's true! Look at him! It says it all over his face, he's about to kill the both of us! That was the plan, this whole time!

What do you think The Boss whispered in his ear before he strolled off, all of a sudden so happy he was whistling? He wasn't whistling so that I wouldn't hear what he said, he didn't want you to hear him dead men tell no tales, Vino! Now shoot his ass, before he shoots you!" Saint Sinner said, practically begging Vino to do something, pretending to sound as desperate as he could.

"NOOOO!" Vino screamed.

Vasquez had just enough time to readjust his gaze, from Saint Sinner to vino, before Vino started unloading his clip, into him, hitting him twice, out of the eight shots fired. Vasquez lay sprawled on the ground, as Vino continued to pull the trigger, a click, click, clicking, and sound coming from the spent clip.

Vino shook the gun, as if to hear if there were any more bullets rattling around inside the gun, before he lunged at the prone Vasquez, climbing on top of him and beating him to a bloody pulp, all the while, screaming things like, "that is what he whispered to you!" and "kill me?!" and "who's smarter now, asshole?"

Saint Sinner swiftly grabbed the spade, holding it with both hands, like a baseball bat, and swung it with every ounce of strength he could muster, at the back of Vino's neck, while he was till preoccupied with Vasquez's beating. The shovel connected with Vino's neck, squarely separating his head from his shoulders. The second swing hit, with a sickening thud, bone crunching and blood spraying.

Vino's lifeless body landed on Vasquez's cooling corpse. Saint Sinner rolled Vino over and relieved him of his knife, then he located Vasquez's revolver, moving as quickly as he could, just in case The Boss was on his way back. He was sure that The Boss had heard the shots. Saint Sinner knelt down, partially hidden by the two bodies. He went to lick his lips and realized that his face, shirt, arms, hands, and everything was covered in Vino's blood.

Saint Sinner shook his head, thinking to himself, "I can't believe I just ingested some scumbag's blood... Almost immediately following that thought, he was overcome by a strange feeling that someone, or something, else was looking through his own eyes.

It felt like he was momentarily sharing his mind with another person. He tried to shake the feeling, but nothing seemed to work. He had more important things to deal with, currently, than a strange feeling, so he checked the revolver, to make sure it was fully loaded, and grabbed a flashlight from the canvas bag. Turning the flashlight on, to make sure it worked, he headed for the entrance to the cave. He was on a mission. He had a score to settle, he needed to finish this once and for all.

It was time to hunt down The Boss. The tables had turned, thanks to a trigger-happy, insecure bad guy, and, now, it was time to track down the top dog. This was it.

The moon was still high in the sky, and very bright, so Saint Sinner was able to use the moonlight to make his way up to, and into, the cave without needing to use his flashlight right away.

He didn't want The Boss to know exactly where he was by giving him a bright-ass light to use as a target. The Boss had to have heard those shots, right? He would know that something had gone awry. The sound from those shots would have traveled for miles, and in the confines of the cave, the noise would have been amplified.

"So much for an ambush," Saint Sinner thought.

He had six shots to tear the soul out of the old bastard who deserved a much slower and more painful death than a bullet could offer. Saint Sinner would use his own hands to do the deed, if he thought he could get away with it. But, he didn't. Better to just shoot the old fuck, and be done with it. "Now, to find that miserable old prick," Saint Sinner thought. He looked around, and back behind him, and noticed the white van. The van was behind him, so that had to mean The Boss was still somewhere deep inside the tunnel network of the cave.

There was a chance the old man had found the other entrance to the cave, but Saint Sinner doubted it. The Boss was just a seventy-two year old man, who was lost in the cave, unprepared. It wouldn't take Saint Sinner long to find him, or so he thought.

He zigzagged his way deeper into the cave, a short burst here and there, from one side to the other. He paused for a moment, hunched down in the dark, with his flashlight and gun at the ready. He took a few deep, slow breaths and continued on his way deeper into the cave. The cave appeared to be made from sandstone, the walls felt smooth and the roof of the cave looked smooth, too.

As he slowly made his way forward, he hoped that luck was with him, he did not want to trip and fall down a crevasse and end up breaking a bone. It was dark, really dark. He held his hand in front of his face, and couldn't see it at all. He had a sneaking suspicion that he'd end up walking into an ambush. He was thinking about how far he'd come, and how much it would suck to end up dying now.

Saint Sinner got to his hands and knees, to reduce the chance of being spotted if, for instance, the old man heard something and shine his light to investigate. His groping fingers felt along the floor. Smooth, just like the walls. It almost had a man-made feel to it. Saint Sinner's eyes were finally beginning to adjust to the dark. He was now able to make out vague shapes in the darkness around him.

He noticed the ramp-like floor of the cave descending down, down, into the darkness. He also took note of the general shape of the cavern he stood in. But, the one thing he was looking for, The Boss, was nowhere to be seen. He was definitely around, somewhere, though. Now, that, Saint Sinner knew for sure.

Now that his eyes had adjusted, he scanned his immediate area for some sort of a clue, and to where the old man could have gone. In doing so, he though he saw something that resembled a footprint, right in front of where he was kneeling. Upon closer inspection, he confirmed it. They were footprints, in the thin layer of sand that blanketed the cave's floor, leading deeper into depths of the dark cave.

Excited about his discovery, Saint Sinner held his breath, in an attempt to hear if The Boss was somewhere close-by. Twenty seconds passed, forty, then a minute. He exhaled quietly and held his breath once again, just to be sure. Nothing. Now he was certain The Boss wasn't too close by. He covered the lens of his flashlight with the palm of his hand, just to play it safe, and flipped the switch to 'on.' Slowly, carefully, he began to uncover the lens, and was able to see the nondescript environment of the cave around him. Navigating through the cave was much easier when there was light enough to see by, it turns out.

Saint Sinner continued his perilous journey, onward down the path. Each step taken was carefully placed.

He listened, smelled the air, and waited. He had been trained to make use of all his senses, and that, he did. Just as he was about to continue moving along, he cocked his head to the side, thinking he heard something in the distance.

It sounded like a soft moaning of sorts, a deep, low, vibrating moan. He didn't know what that humming, moaning sound could possibly be, but it didn't sound human at all. "There's something alien down here, something strange," he thought. He felt it more than he thought it, it seemed. Immediately, he started to silently berate himself for even entertaining the idea of something alien living in the cave. It was nonsense, and he knew it. He knew better than to jump at shadow like a teenager. Just then, he thought he had it figured out. The wind. The wind was, most likely, the cause of the moaning sound. Saint Sinner shook his head, smiling at the ridiculousness of the whole situation.

He adjusted the long-handled flashlight, in his hand, and swept the beam of light from the left to the right, slowly, inspecting every crack, gap, and shift in the sand. "Where the fuck did the old man go?" he thought, once again. The path narrowed down to the size of a sidewalk. The cave's walls rose about six meters from the floor, or close to it, and the smoothly arched ceiling continued far, out of sight.

The flashlight's beam pierced the darkness, revealing a cone-shaped slice of cavern to his already straining eyes.

The light stretched far ahead, all the way until the tunnel bottlenecked, and took a sharp turn to the right, concealing everything further from view. There had been no other branches, or forks, offering additional options for escaping, or hiding in. It was all one tunnel so far. There was nowhere else to go. The old man had to be up ahead. Perhaps he was waiting just around the corner, knowing that Saint Sinner would follow.

Pausing, Saint Sinner considered his options. He could turn away now, and leave. Just take the van, and drive away. The odds of the old bastard surviving out here, without food or water, under the blazing sun and the heat of the desert days, and the freezing nighttime temperatures, weren't very good.

Add to that the fact that he would have to walk his limping-ass sixty miles to the nearest civilization, and that virtually made his odds nonexistent. He thought about driving there, to the nearest town, and sitting there, waiting patiently in the local diner, eating cake or pie, and drinking coffee, for some ragged, shambled, form to manifest itself from the shimmering heat of the desert.

Then he could just drive his van toward the figure, point the front end at the old bastard, and put the pedal to the metal. The Boss would lay broken, and torn, defeated after an extreme struggle. A smile split Saint Sinner's face at the thought. It would be great to do, but Saint Sinner knew he would never go that route.

No, he never left things unfinished. It was against his personal code of conduct to do that. He'd wait here, slowly creep his way around the corner ahead, and hope that McCracken wasn't on the other side waiting for him, ready to blast his ass. He would fight and kill the man, just like he'd done so many times before, on other jobs, and then he'd go and collect the bounty. After that, he'd be getting ready to do it all over again. Or, maybe he'd retire. He was still young enough to start a family. He had put in his time, and made his bones. After the cash-out on this job, there really wasn't much he couldn't do. A pretty wife, two point five kids.

They could live a life of luxury for the remainder of their days.

Saint Sinner smiled that face-splitting, euphoric smile again, but it wasn't long before it was replaced by a disappointed grimace. He knew he wouldn't be doing any of those things, either. He'd keep on doing what he's always done. One day, he knew, he'd meet a challenge that he wouldn't be able to overcome, and he would die. As he lay there, dying, he'd regretfully think about how he had the chance to stop sooner, and had decided not to. He'd think about the family that he could have had, and should have, had, and then it would be all over.

Snapping back to reality, and the task at hand, he reached into his pocket and removed a few coins.

Gun ready, he whipped some of the coins around the corner, causing them to bounce, as they struck the walls and floor, and make all sorts of clinking noises and rattling pings.

Saint Sinner, listening for any sound or indication that The Boss was around, held the gun out, ready to fire. He waited, but there was nothing. He then tossed the remaining coins, and again, listened, hoping for some sort of a reaction. Still nothing.

His stomach in knots, and his heart hammering in his chest, he mentally began to prepare himself. He didn't like the situation, but he had to work with what he had. He had to see what was on the other side of that corner. He had to. Unfortunately, without a mirror, he'd have to physically check to see what laid in waiting for him. He took a deep breath, bracing himself.

He was ready to move.

A moan broke the silence.

The sound was low and deep.

It definitely wasn't the wind. It wasn't the natural sound that he'd told himself it was earlier. That strange feeling came back again, stronger than before, like there was somebody trapped between his eyes, watching him, reading his thoughts. For some reason he felt as if the presence was trying to warn him of something this time, though, his instincts hinted at impending danger.

The hair on his arms, and neck, stood on end and panic raced through him. The same feeling a young child feels, when he or she know, is absolutely sure, that there is a monster under their bed, hiding there, and waiting. A terrible monster with razor-sharp claws and needle fangs that wants nothing more than to kill.

A foreboding sense of dread washed over him, like a wave. Somewhere in the darkness, something was closing in on him, and he could feel it. He briefly looked down at the flashlight in his hand, then out at the small circle of light it cast against the wall opposite him. He shook his head, and fingered the trigger of the revolver in his other hand nervously.

He thought to himself, "Here goes nothing," and he quickly sprang from where he was standing and bolted around the corner. He was ready for action, his muscles tensed and his nerves were drawn tight, like a wire pulled to its limits and about to snap. "Motherfucker!" he said to himself, quietly, trying to keep his heart from beating out of his chest.

Saint Sinner was relieved to see the carved out passage continuing on, into a much larger, more open chamber of sorts, instead of the old prick, smiling, just as he pulled the trigger.

He aimed the flashlight all around to inspect the new area. Here was much like the rest of the tunnel, but the ceiling and floor had stalactites and stalagmites everywhere, and there was bat shit all over the place.

The large chamber, up ahead, sort of resembled the gaping maw of a hungry beast. Saint Sinner just realized something he probably should have much sooner than this. He could have kicked himself for being so careless. Here he was, shining the flashlight here, there, and everywhere with the big, open cavern still up ahead. What if The Boss was hiding in that chamber?

Nothing says "here I am" more than a beam of light, leading right back to the person dumb enough to be holding the damn thing, in a pitch-black cave. He quickly flicked off his flashlight, disappointment written all over his face, even though it was, now, too dark to be seen by anyone who could have been there. Next, he lay down flat on the ground, gun held at the ready, letting his eyes readjust to the darkness before making his way forward, crawling along the sandy stone.

In his mind, Saint Sinner figured that if McCracken was actually hiding in the antechamber, then he had a pretty good idea as to where Saint Sinner was now, thanks to the handy-dandy flashlight, and that wasn't good to think about.

The tunnel that Saint Sinner was lying in was very narrow, and relatively straight. All the Boss would have to do is stand at the end, where the tunnel actually connects to the cavern, and pop off a few shots in Saint Sinner's general direction.

There was nowhere to hide, or to take cover, and he'd more than likely end up with a few holes in him that he didn't want, need, or ask for, courtesy of that old bastard, Al. in reality, the only defense Saint Sinner really had was the darkness itself. He had hoped to avoid getting shot, the bullets passing harmlessly overhead, by crawling low to the ground and thinking outside of the box. It wasn't much, but it was all that he had, so he had to make it work.

Minutes passed and he literally inched forward. Saint Sinner estimated it must have taken him nearly half an hour to close the gap between the corner, where he started, and the entrance to the antechamber. During his time spent crawling, he had hoped to hear something that would give away the location, or even the presence, of The Boss, but the only noise he heard was that low-sounding moan, twice, and nothing else.

Without any other logical options left, he continued to make his way past the border, and into the big, open, chamber. After a few tense, quiet moments, he changed positions from prone, to a more comfortable crouch, the flashlight and pistol still at the ready.

He waited for a short while longer, allowing his heart rate to drop. Once it had, he steeled himself, said a silent prayer, and flicked his flashlight back on. The chamber was immense, much bigger than he thought it would be, he was impressed. There were several prominent ledges along the walls, for as far as the feeble light his flashlight's beam generated would allow him to see. Beyond its beam, dark shapes loomed in the shadows, more ledges, and some other cave-like adornments, no doubt.

He held his breath as the flashlight illuminated whatever he pointed it at, as it danced to the left and to the right, all around him. He could smell the dankness of the musty air, as he stayed crouched down, listening, draining his ears to listen. "What the fuck?! What the fuck was that?" he thought, his heart racing once again…

Saint Sinner, once again, killed the light, hoping it wasn't too late to save his ass. He laid all the way back down again, trying to reduce the size of the available target that he had just put out there for anyone to see.

Motionless, he held his breath and listened. A minute passed. Another. Yet another sixty seconds, or so, went by, and not so much as a peep.

He breathing and heart slowly became more normal. It was nothing he told himself. Sometimes darkness plays tricks on the mind, he knew this, it's happened to him before.

He felt comfortable to return to the crouching stance, and then he started to think, "Could the old man have, somehow, hidden himself at the cave's entrance? Was the bastard gone, did he leave just before my arrival? Or, did he flee once he heard Vino fire his gun?

If he managed to back-track to the van... He'd definitely be far, far, away from her by now, and he'd have his grimy goons on their way to come get me."

He briefly thought about his imaginary scenario he came up with earlier in the day, where he sat at the diner in the closest town eating pie, and he thought about the shoe being on the other foot, The Boss waiting for him, just to run him down, after an arduous trek across miles and miles of desert.

Being this deep in the cave, he'd never be able to hear the van's engine, or the sound of it taking off. It was a late model Ford, and ran surprisingly quiet, as it was.

He shook his head to try and rid himself of that awful idea. Now that the immediate danger had come and gone, or what he had thought was immediate danger anyway, he flicked the light back on, and ran it across the large area around him.

It was then, that the light ran across the wall that held her. The massive cave-painting could have been produced by the native cave dwellers of the area, though something about that didn't seem quite right to Saint Sinner, not at all. Even thinking about that being the situation, his stomach began to roll with the 'wrongness' of it, suggesting such a thing seemed to be a grave insult in itself.

Red, black, and white hues were spread over the stone medium, in broad strokes. The art was in some places, vague, and loose, and other, it was chillingly precise, as if it were the work of one of the latest inkjet printers, rather than a hand and archaic brushes, however long ago.

The artwork reached forty feet up, to the ceiling, and depicted what could have been Hindu gods with multiple arms, holding all manner of weapons and tools.

Added to these, were myriad other religious and mythical figures, some widely known, others obscure. All of the figures were portrayed standing in a huge circle, all surrounding on gargantuan figure in the middle of the ring. A woman of extreme, dark beauty, and perfection.

Hell, such was the extent of perfection that his unknown artist portrayed, that Saint Sinner jumped back involuntary, as his light passed over the woman, because, for a moment, he thought he was staring at a real, living and breathing, giant woman in a flowing black dress.

Her face was pale, flawless, like the surface of the moon on a clear, winter night. Her eyes were dark pools, solid, with no pupils, and a malevolent look in them, meant for any and all below her. At the edges of his vision, the shadows seemed to dance impossibly while they were under the steady light of his flashlight. But, apparently nobody informed the shadows that what they were doing was impossible, because dance, they did, giving the impression that the woman moved amid a flutter of dark robes.

Pentagrams, upside-down crucifixes, hammers, Nordic runes, stars, zodiac signs, small words written in, what looked like, every alphabet and language ever conceived, runes, Theban sigils, and more circled the powerful looking woman. Saint Sinner had a feeling that what he was looking at was very, very, old.

Potentially predating the Bronze Age, and maybe even predating man himself, although that made little sense to him.

Everything one could conjure to mind, when trying to describe the magnificence of the powerful deity, fell short. All the marks, carvings, and sigils, looked like many different hands, mediums, colors, and tools were used to create them. It was as if the work had been added to over the millennia. It was obvious that none of the work had been exclusively produced in any single era. All the evidence pointed to the opposite.

Saint Sinner shined his light across the wall again, and this time he noticed some sort of astrological-looking symbols. These weren't depictions of, say, a bull representing Taurus. This looked like a map of the stars, whole constellations were depicted in magnificent detail. This was the kind of stuff that lore spoke of. There were rings around the constellations, and what looked like expanding dimensions, making their way out and across, what Saint Sinner thought was, the universe. There was one, in particular, that reminded him of the Milky Way galaxy, great swirling strokes created a whirlpool-like design.

It also looked like the solar system, we know and love, could be seen on the outer arm of one of the swirls. Saint Sinner took his attention away from the stunning display, and looked back at the painting of the goddess.

For the first time, he noted a mark on the open palm of her right hand that almost looked like it could be a small, black pearl, or something like it. It was round, dark, and hungry looking.

The mark could have been just about anything: a doll, a ball, a marble. But, Saint Sinner didn't think any of those things were likely to be accurate. After a few moments of contemplation, the answer finally came to him. He didn't know how he knew, he just knew. It was a black hole, it had to be, and that would make sense, considering all the astrological references and drawings.

In the other hand of the goddess, she held the Earth as if it were hers, like she owned it. On the Earth, there were dotted lines that intersected at certain longitudinal and latitudinal coordinates. There was also a nautical looking compass. By the looks of it, some mathematical genius had gone ahead and mapped out important locations on the painted Earth, but what were they for?

Locations of what?

Saint Sinner rubbed his temples, while he tried to think back, to remember what it was The Boos had said earlier in the day. It didn't take him long to recall The Boss saying something about doorways, or portals to another world.

But, that was just a rumor, a myth. It had to be, right? Well, that could explain why he wasn't able to find the old man, maybe he opened a door to another world, and.... No, that was impossible. Saint Sinner disregarded the idea, dismissed it as nonsensical.

The cold, hard orbs of the goddess's eyes looked down on Saint Sinner, they held no emotion, unaffected by thousands of years spent waiting in the dark, experiencing the change from strife and conflict to elation and back again, maybe even seeing a sacrifice or two in that time, too.

With those eyes locked on him, he couldn't help but think about how new, how fresh the paint still looked after all that time spent in the dark, musty cave. It had probably been there for thousands upon thousands of years, but it looked as if it had been painted that very day.

Every time he would divert his attention elsewhere, he felt compelled, almost, to look back at her, to stare. He found it harder and harder to look away, as the shadows danced around her head, her wild, ebony strands of hair mingling with the flowing black of the robes she wore, embraced by the darkness surrounding her, the void of the universe.

A series of, what could have been runes stood out to Saint Sinner, that he hadn't noticed before, resembling the wheel of the zodiac. He started to feel as though he was being swallowed up, as he took another look at the multitude of symbols, it was all so overwhelming.

Another ancient symbol, the black sun, caught his eye. Saint Sinner recognized that black sun. He'd seen it before, but where? A book? A painting? No, it was in a series of photographs from the First World War. The black sun is set, behind the golden sun, its light invisible to the physical world. It represents the vortex, the passageway, to another dimension.

"Black holes..." he thought to himself, "even light bends to the will of such power. It's unable to resist. Entire planets and constellations are lured in, and eaten alive. Time itself stops and funnels through currents, connected to an altogether different place and time. The queen of death, goddess of the universe entire. She appeared ready to step out, into the cavern.

Saint Sinner shone his light on the floor of the cavern, right in front of the painted wall, to find an intricate black sun staring back at him. There were shallow-looking trenches that led away from the sun that were stained by something rust-colored from long, long, ago.

His gut told him that he knew what the stains most likely were, blood.

He all of a sudden felt very uneasy. "Sacrifice...To me...Centuries... Millennia... I am the demi-god, guardian of this portal...kill for me," a faint whisper.

Saint Sinner took a step back, looking over his shoulder, before he aimed the flashlight up into the face of the goddess, "What the hell was that?" he said to himself quietly, shaken by the whisper from an unknown source.

Looking up at the painting, he was awestruck all over again. He thought about how the painting was the last thing the poor sacrificed people would ever set their eyes on before the knife swiftly flashed down, ending their existence and draining their blood, watching it fill the trenches of the black sun on the ground. It was almost as if time and space had become one in this chamber, it was an odd feeling.

Speaking of odd feelings, Saint Sinner booked up into the eyes of the goddess, and for a moment, he felt like they were actually staring back into his own. Just like that, that uncanny feeling was back upon him, that same presence as before. It was an invasion of his body, his mind, and it was unsettling. It wasn't as if the presence was making demands, or anything, but he found himself walking into the center of the black sun. He felt like he was in a dream, or a trance.

That deep, low moaning sound came from every direction, all at once, it emanated from the cavern itself. For whatever reason, Saint Sinner felt, all of a sudden, compelled to lay down, grab Vino's knife, and slit his throat with a single, deep slash, letting his life blood splash down into the trenches at this feet.

He withdrew the knife, he wanted to honor himself for her, an overwhelming urge to sacrifice himself washed over him. He raised the blade, high above his head, and closed his eyes. He tensed his muscles, and was about to take the plunge, when booming laughter came from somewhere nearby, snapping Saint Sinner out of it.

He dropped the knife on the ground, shook himself violently, unbelieving what he was just about to do, and shined the flashlight all over, quickly, trying to pinpoint the source of the laughter, as the voice he'd been hearing in his head receded into the unknown, from which it came.

"Well, now, lad, you look a little woozy, if I do say so myself. It looks, to me, like you've lost your marbles. If I hadn't seen what I just saw, with my own two eyes, I never would've believed it," more throaty laughter ensued.

"What were you just doing, there, before I interrupted? Certainly, I know what it looked like you were doing, lad, but I seem to be having a hard time wrapping my head around it," The Boss's voice echoed off the walls of the chamber, making it nearly impossible to hone in on the source.

Saint Sinner, still off balance, and slightly confused, was barraged by strange visions. As if being watched through the eyes of another, he saw his own death taking place. The vision was so vivid.

There he was, kneeling in the center of the black sun on the chamber's floor, the knife held high above his head, his knuckles white from gripping the hilt. Down the knife came, in a flashing arc, from right to left slashing both his jugular and carotid artery. He could see himself topple over, to the side, lying sprawled across the floor, in a morbid semblance of one who was trying to make a snow angel, but instead of snow there was only sand and blood.

Blood that he could see himself choking on. Blood that was gushing from him, thick and crimson. It flowed from him as if it had no intention of ever stopping. His hands, chest, and stomach, were painted red by it, and the puddle grew larger beneath his body, as it worked its way outward, flowing into the trenches carved into the black sun. Saint Sinner watched on, as the light in his own eyes, the very essence of his being, grew dim and faded away to nothing, as his life drained from the gaping wound in his neck.

The experience was so real, so life-like, that Saint Sinner became overwhelmed by it all, in his panic, he clenched his fists, forgetting about the gun in his hand. "Bang! Bang! Bang! Bang! Bang! Bang!" Six shots, fired in rapid succession, uselessly hit the ground.

"Click! Click! Click!"

Again, The Boss's laughter filled the cavern, snapping Saint Sinner out of the reverie of a bad trip he seemed to be having. Too late, he had just realized what he had done. All his rounds spent, he no longer had the protection of the revolver.

Just then, The Boss stepped out from behind a mass of rocky stalagmites, no more than ten yards from where Saint Sinner had been the entire time. "Almost, lad!" he said, chuckling. "I'm surprised, shooting like that, you didn't end up catching one of those in the foot.

Now, I'm trying to make sense of this all, so bear with me, here. So, here we have a tough guy contract killer, tough as nails, always calm and collected, who apparently has lost his nerve. If I didn't know any better, I'd go as far as to say that you were afraid, scared like a wee-little girl?

And to top it off, you fire every single round at your disposal into the ground...Nobody would believe me, if I told them about his. Hell, lad, even I wouldn't believe me."

The Boss looked up at the painted deity on the cavern wall, her, in all her glory, and then set his sights back on Saint Sinner, whose eyes were already, and had been locked on him.

The Boss had his pistol pointed right at Saint Sinner, from the thirty, or so, feet away, and slowly, carefully began to walk toward him. All the thoughts, of sacrifice, and visions, of himself dying, had fled as his mind cleared up. Now, his concern was the old man with a gun who was walking toward him. But, be that as it may, Saint Sinner still had to fight the urge to look back at the painting of the goddess.

The pull that compelled him to look was strong, too strong. He-had-to-look. He shined his flashlight up the face on the wall, his mouth slightly agape. Even The Boss sneaked a quick glance at her, as he continued to walk toward him.

"Aye, she reminds me of a lass I knew back home, in Ireland. Old Miss Foley, she, too, was big and dumb looking. Had those same dark eyes, and a blank expression to match. About as smart as that, there, rock she's painted on," The Boss said, smiling. A second or two passed, passed before he continued, "After she would pleasure me, I'd slap her. Not no ordinary, run-of-the-mill slap either. I'd slap her silly, lad. Sometimes until she'd bleed. She like it too. Liked to get slapped so hard it would make her head spin, make her dizzy. There'd be handprints all over her pale, freckled skin."

Saint Sinner was hardly listening to anything The Boss was saying, he was too drawn to the painting to pay much attention or anything else. "And then, right before she'd leave, I'd walk her to the door.

Well, to the top of the stairs, anyway. I'd plant my foot in her ass and push her down them. I'd kick that wench as hard, and as fast, as I could." he laughed, "She wouldn't always fall down the stairs, though you know. Sometimes she would. Eventually, the boys began placing bets as to whether she'd fall or not. Her falling wasn't a rare occurrence, by any means," the Boss shook his head, still smiling, "she'd pick herself up off the ground, mouth full of dirt and mud, sometimes blood, and she'd still turn back around and smile at me before she started her seven-mile trek home. The boys even flavored the mud for her, sometimes. They started pissing at the foot of the stairs, "the Boss's laughter was loud, as he slapped his knee.

Saint Sinner was still being pulled toward that painting, but he managed to focus on The Boss for a moment.

"You know it rains more often than not in Ireland, and seven miles is a long way to walk in the rain, but she would do the same thing every week. She came by, letting me curse at her, and abuse her any way I'd please. Do you have any idea why that was, lad? Any at all? "The Boss asked.

Saint Sinner lowered his gaze from the goddess to meet the eyes of The Boss. "I'll tell you why... Because, to her, I was fucking god. That's why. She did what I said to do, anything at all, without question. They all did, all of them, because they knew that if they didn't, they'd have to face the wrath of this God.

I'd come down on them with a rage that would shake the very pillars of creation. The devil, himself, would be impressed, "The Boss said. He turned his attention back to the goddess of the cavern, clearly not worried about Saint Sinner making a move, or even the possibility.

"I raced further into the cave, right after I heard the shot you fired, and stumbled upon this cavern, and the paintings. At first, I thought to myself, wondering why some idiot would be in here drawing on the walls.

Obviously, it had to have been some simple fool who'd done it. I figured they probably got into a bad batch of mushrooms, or something, while they were out wandering around, picking their nose and generally making a nuisance of himself, you know, like the simple-minded fools generally do. Now, look, this moron's come and used bat shit to paint this stinking whore on the wall.

She does remind me, a lot, of my Margaret, though. Maybe I could go on up and slap her, for old time's sake what do you think about that, lad? The Boss laughed heartily, shaking his head in remembrance of the good old days. "Oh, Margaret, where has the time gone?" he seemed to say to himself.

"Looking at this abomination on the wall, the smug look on her face, like she owns the damn place, makes me sick," he said. "I've the mind to hire a crew and redecorate, paint over this pagan Mona Lisa, here, and have a likeness of me self-put up, instead." The Boss looked as though he were actually considering doing just that, then he muttered something that sounded like, "… could have been Harry Potter's mother."

Just then, another vision forced its way into the mind of Saint Sinner. This time, he saw himself wearing a flowing black robe, similar to the one worn by the goddess, standing over The Boss's wrinkly, old, naked body. He had been bound and placed at the center of the black sun, his old saggy skin hanging and covered in welts and bruises. This hand, Saint Sinner held a commercial dagger, of sorts, arm outstretched above his head.

He stood there, with the blade held high, for just a moment before he drove the blade home, with all of his strength, aiming the blade, with deadly accuracy, at the suffering old man's blackened, vicious heart.

The old man, once the most feared, infamous villain, was now little more than a pitiful, weak, shaken old fool who was about to die. The Boss opened his mouth, terror in his eyes, and pathetically screamed in protest, seeming to wither away, even before the blade had struck.

Through the dream-like vision, it tore, dragging Saint Sinner out of his murderous fancies and back to the present, to the room, to the gun pointed at him, and to his enemy who held it.

Again, the presence inside of him, that voice screamed, "Danger!"

The voice hadn't been warning him about the old man, or even about the painting, it had been trying to warn him about the sudden danger that loomed from behind him. Too late.

Slam! The stock of a gun met the back of his neck, right on the nerves that control balance and other important things like that. Saint Sinner collapsed.

He slammed the floor, his head spinning out of control. He managed to stay conscious, but he almost wished he hadn't. He was the recipient of a violent kick to the kidney, which was delivered, first class, by the Marlboro man, himself, Vasquez. Saint Sinner instantly pissed his pants, as if the "flush" button had been pressed on his bladder.

Again, the butt end of the rifle fell upon the poor Saint Sinner, but this time it hit him in the skull, and rattled his brain. Nauseating waves of pain washed over him. He could feel the warmth of his own blood flowing over his face. The third, and final blow that he happened to be awake enough to feel, brought his world from full screen, to a pinhole. He teetered on the brink, about to fall into the abyss.

Vasquez flicked on a small, battery-powered Coleman lamp. To say the little lamp was bright would be an understatement, the brilliant white light flooded the cavern with a pale, glowing luminescence. He carefully set the lamp on the floor, right beside the growing pool of Saint Sinner's blood. Vasquez began to speak, and when he did, his voice was clear and sounded fresh, like he was relaxed, he said, "So long Sinner, see you in hell." He shook his head, staring down at Saint Sinner with disappointment in his eyes, "I can't believe you didn't put a couple more holes in me, just for good measure, you know, to make sure the dead guys were really dead?" Vasquez chuckled quietly before continuing, "I know I would have had to make sure. To think you're a professional, too! He laughed at that.

"You, honestly, didn't wonder why I wasn't leading. It never even crossed your mind, really? Well, I suppose with Vino's stupid ass, which most certainly was bleeding profusely, on top of me, it would have been rather difficult to pick up on. I can understand that. I owe my life to this, here, bulletproof vest," he slapped his chest to indicate where one might wear such a vest, "and, unfortunately, for you, the mistake you made is going to cost you, and Sinner, it was mighty expensive, too."

Vasquez grinned, thinking himself clever. He towered over Saint Sinner, a pensive look about him, he said, "I was just thinking..." he reached down and picked up Vino's knife that Saint Sinner had dropped, "You and me, we're going to have some fun, buddy." He turned the knife in his hands, inspecting the blade. "I think I'm going to use this, in the name of Vino, of course. He'd like that."

A sadistic smile slithered across Vasquez's face, as he thought about all the possibilities. He pulled a lighter from one of his pockets, flipping it between his fingers.

It took Saint Sinner a moment to realize that he had lost consciousness for some time, he looked around and tried to stand, but that was when he realized that he couldn't. He was bound, hand, and foot, and was placed in the center of the big black sun on the ground. The thought had just registered about it being light in the cavern, and not only that, but Vasquez appeared to be alive, well, and standing beside him with a lighter. "Not good, not good at all," he thought.

A flicking noise could be heard, as the lighter lit up, a small flame danced around and cast faint shadows as it moved closer.

A shooting, stinging pain flared up through his leg as the flame touched his skin, instantly bubbling up the flesh. The smell of scorched hair and skin assaulted his nose.

Saint Sinner struggled and fought, twisting, and turning every-which-way, trying desperately to loosen, slip, or break his restraints before the pain broke him. He struggled and fought in vain. Apparently, Lady Luck was on her lunch break. The smell was terrible, and it grew stronger still, reminding him of active duty. Reminding him of the aftermath of a terrorist attack, the bodies pulled from the rubble of a building that had been bombed, broken, missing limbs, charred, blackened, and skin. It was the smell of death.

Saint Sinner had to do something. He had to find a way to stop the pain. He bit down on his lip, hard, trying to distract himself from the hellish pain he was experiencing at the hands of

Vasquez.

He thought he might be able to focus on the pain in his lip, in order to focus less on the fact that he was slowly being burned alive. No matter what happened, though, no matter what these two son-of-bitches decided to put him through, he decided that would-not-be giving them the satisfaction of hearing him scream out in pain.

"You see, lad, crime does pay," The Boss said, smiling and watching from a distance, "and in the end, the bad guys do win. Always have. Always will."

Vasquez cocked his head, his eyes lowering to Saint Sinner's feet, as he brought the flame from one, already toasted, toe to another. The all-to-familiar sizzle and flare sent another excruciating wave of pain through Saint Sinner. A blister popped, just like a child poking a bubble, and a clear liquid seeped from the wound. The liquid flashed when it hit the flame, like water hitting a grease-covered skillet.

Sweat poured from Saint Sinner's forehead, as the pain became more and more intense. Vasquez was cooking him alive, one inch at a time, with his red Bic lighter.

The Boss, standing still as a statue, was watching the expression on Saint Sinner's face, as blood started to trickle down his chin from his teeth biting into, and through, his lip. Still, he refused to scream.

Every muscle ached, every nerve in his body seemed to be screaming for him. His body flipped, spun, tossed, and turned in his struggle to not scream out.

This experience was, by far, the worse pain he had ever felt. He was both surprised and disappointed that he hadn't passed out yet. The torturous waves kept rolling through him, vast, deep, and bitter cold.

Vasquez worked his way across all ten of his toes before moving on to the soft, sensitive flesh on Saint Sinner's calf muscle. He let the flame flicker his knee cap, on the backside, where the soft fold of skin burning brought a whole new meaning to the word pain.

Saint Sinner managed to pry his eyes open and look up at the goddess on the wall. She had those ebony eyes that were cruel, menacing, and all-knowing. They seemed to be peering back at him, into his very soul. He held her gaze without blinking, as sweat dropped off his face and onto the floor. His hands, thrashed open and closed, and his legs pumped back and forth.

He was in agony.

He was forced to use all his willpower, everything he had learned over the years, to not scream out. He shook sweat, spit, and blood from his face, but still he managed to focus on those two bottomless, black pools.

In his mind he called out to her, a desperate, angry outburst, and "Do you like what you see? Are you happy, now?! Here is your pound of flesh, your sacrifice! I am yours, here, now, in this God-forsaken cave, forgotten by time! I die for you! My pain is all for you! I scream not for my enemy, but for you, alone! It's all for you! and for what?

What, for my sacrifice?

For my strength, my devotion?

What, in return?"

Saint Sinner was delirious with pain, as Vasquez decided to change things up, to keep things interesting. He started to say something, no doubt, meant to strike fear into the heart of Saint Sinner, but it had no effect.

Saint Sinner was too far gone to be listening to him ramble. He didn't hear a word of it. Nor did he notice as the first slice of skin was flayed from his shin.

Vasquez grabbed ahold of the strip of skin that had been sliced by Vino's knife, with a leather man's pliers, and literally tore the flesh from Saint Sinner's bones. Vasquez worked its way around one leg, and then went to work on the other. All the while, Saint Sinner locked eyes with the goddess on the wall, her eyes held his gaze.

The Boss took a seat, smiling serenely, clearly enjoying the show. Saint Sinner's head was pinned against the ancient floor, fixed in position, looking up at the queen of darkness above him. Something looked different about the paint, it looked wet, freshly coated.

There were spots that dripped downward in rivulets. Her face seemed even more flawless than before, beautiful, perfect.

Now, Saint Sinner was hovering in the air, above his own body, looking down at it. He no longer felt the feeble attempts of Vasquez. The Boss got up and walked over. He stood right next to Saint Sinner's head.

He leaned down, and he followed his line of sight.

He sneered, and glared at the goddess on the wall before looking back at Saint Sinner, "I see what you're doing, lad. I have to admit, as much as I hate your fucking guts, I have to admire a man that can focus enough to withstand this kind of pain. It's impressive. You've cheated me out of my fun, lad, by inducing this half-assed, hippy trance upon yourself." He shook his head, frowning.

"So, you lock eyes with the whore on the wall, and everything is okay? Is that how it works?"

"What did you do, offer yourself to her for help, or something?"

"Is she helping you, lad?" the Boss glanced at her once again, and in one fluid motion, pulled out his revolver.

"Did she speak to you, tell you everything was going to be okay? Tell you that we'll be letting you go at the end? Did she, now, lad?" the Boss glanced, a second time, up at the wall, this time he looked her dead in the eyes before turning his attention back on Saint Sinner, "Well, lad, if she told you all that nonsense, she damn-well lied to you," he laughed a cruel laugh.

"It'll be just the opposite, for you.

Death is all that you have to look forward to now, and there be nothing your painted friend can do to stop it. This is MY will, what I command is law! I am god, here!"

The Boss swung his arm up and shot two rounds into the piece of goddess on the wall.

Vasquez jumped up, grinning.

"I am the giver of life and the bringer of death! I have the final say as to whether you live or die, lad. She can look at you all she wants, and you her, but I say nothing will come of it!"

The Boss raised his arm, once again, he pointed his gun right at Saint Sinner, point-blank. The Boss quickly angled the gun away from Saint Sinner and popped off three more shots, the blasts echoing off the walls, and the bullets ricocheting into the shadows.

"I don't have much time, lad. I've got to go. For, I have castles to conquer and kings to kill. This is where your time on Earth comes to an end.

You will know, here and now, in this shit-hole cave that and the whore on the wall is nothing more than that, a whore on a wall.

"She is no goddess!" he said.

"She is nothing but a peyote-induced cave painting. She couldn't stop me from farting, let alone stop me from killing you," The Boss laughed maniacally, "there is only one God, here!" he glared at Saint Sinner, as he continued to play out the last words. He aimed his pistol at

Saint Sinner's head, "... and that mother fucking God is ME!"

The Boss winked and pulled the trigger. The blast tore through Saint Sinner's left eye, exploding the socket, and mutilating the brain behind it. Saint Sinner's world had come to an end, and he was grateful for it.

All life had left Shamus Quinn, once known as Saint Sinner, the spotless military career, the contract killing, his entire being had been exhaled into the ancient cave, under the close supervision of Helena, queen of the dead and gate keeper of time and space. She was the spirit of the void, the black hole connecting our galaxy to the universe. The Boss had entered her sanctuary and defiled her name, denounced her power.

He had attempted to sacrifice in his own name on the hallowed, sacred ground that belonged to her. His temerity had awoken her from her eternal slumber.

She was awake and angry. She took away his power, watched him leave, and set forth a balancing force.

Blackness.

Saint Sinner knew blackness.

He was conscious and aware of it without feeling the need for his body. There was no breath, no pulse, and no blood coursing through his veins.

He remembered.

He had been sacrificed, left on the floor of the ancient cave. He remembered all the symbols. He remembered her eyes. Death had its advantages. Rest, plenty of time for rest. Awareness.

How was it possible?

Awareness of self, without self?

He was considering this, when he saw movement. A small pinprick of white. A dot, it was growing, and it glowed like a distant star. It grew to the size of a headlight, then he was able to see more.

Black, flowing, and swirling though out the whiteness. Robes. Hair. Arms. Eyes.

Time and space seemed to be carrying her, moving her along. Closer, now, she had come off the wall and stood before him. Speaking thoughts into his awareness. Black eyes, and lips the color of dead roses, the only one that mattered.

Her voice was not sound, but earthquakes of vibration, the whispers of the Earth. She breathed him back into existence. Into his body.

"I am Hel, the goddess of death, born of Loki and Angerboda. I hail from Helheim, under a root of the World Tree, Yggdrasil. I am Mimir's twin sister, evolved from the ancient race of giants. I am the guardian of sacred, mystic treasure. A being of supreme power, given knowledge by Wotan, I am the guardian of the door to the nine realms. I give your life renewed.

Death, without my blessing, means nothing.

He can no more force it than he could grow wings and fly. Such things are not for those like him. Seek revenge upon him and his. Bathe in their blood, drink your fill, and glut yourself from their crushed skulls. Only when my throat is quenched, shall you be set free. Rise, guest, for I grant your life with my kiss of death."

A kiss, she blew from her lips, and out came the breath of life, from death. "You are my reaper. Vengeance is your new mission. Go forth!" Saint Sinner sat up, drawing in a deep, gasping, breath, his first, since his last, thirteen minutes prior. He found himself comfortable in the surrounding darkness and silence, the musty, dank smell of deep-earth all around him. Seeing things through his left eye was different.

He could see things in tints of red, like he was looking through a filter, and darkness, apparently, meant nothing. He knew it was dark, yet he could see a rat nibbling on a piece of his discarded flesh.

All of a sudden, he was more parched than he had ever been.

He needed a drink, and he needed one, now. Instinct welled up inside of him, too fast to stop, he snatched the unsuspecting rodent up, snapped its neck with a twist, and tore its head clear off.

Next thing he knew, he held the lifeless body of the rat upside down, above his lips, drinking its blood. As the blood entered Saint Sinner's body, a vision flashed through his mind, gone almost before it began.

It was The Boss walking, followed by Vasquez. They hopped into the white van and drove away, without a second look back. They didn't even pay vino's corpse any mind before leaving. Saint Sinner's legs, fresh from death, were healed. Scarred over. The gruesome wounds that had been afflicted, had all been marked out in darkness, the blackest-looking ink imaginable. The same black as the color of her eyes. The tattoos marking the sites of his torturous treatment, were the only evidence of the deadly acts that had taken his life.

Saint Sinner ran his hand over the scar where his left eye had been. The smooth skin, covering the socket, provided no hindrance to his newly gained sight. He retained normal vision in his right eye. Looking through his left eye was like looking at sun with your eyes closed. Flexing his limbs, he felt stronger that he had ever been. He walked out of the cave and saw night came alive in every direction. The desert air was cooler, and more welcoming than he could remember.

Bright, and full, was the moon, surrounded by a breathtaking blanket of stars. Saint Sinner looked longingly at the entrance to the cave.

Faintly, he could hear the song of the goddess. Ancient was he worship. He wasn't afraid. He knew she held him in the palm of her hand.

He nodded to her before walking over to where the fresh tire tracks in the sand led off toward the distant lights. He followed with his eyes, then with his feet.

With his first step, he knew what he intended to do.

It was what he was good at.

She knew it too and pulled the strings to his body with laughter.

He would kill, against his will.

She would never stop.

Did he have a choice?

To be continued...

Made in the USA
Middletown, DE
09 May 2023

29788776R00142